COYOTE WHISPERS

COYOTE HUNGER BOOK 3

RHIAN CAHILL

Coyote Whispers
Coyote Hunger Book 3
By Rhian Cahill

For more information visit:
www.rhiancahill.com

*Alan, I know they're not kangaroo shifters but this one's for you.
Billi and her invaluable snow info and the Heat Wave readers
for the drywall.
Fedora, thank you for keeping me in line.
Mr. C, I love you more with every day. Together Forever.*

*I'd like to give a special thank you to all the readers of the Coyote
Hunger series. Without you and your demands for more I
wouldn't have written Doc and Steve's story so soon. Thank you
from the bottom of my heart for loving the members of the
Whispering Mountains coyote pack as much as I do.*

1

MAY EIGHTEENTH

STEVE SAT ENCLOSED by darkness and listened to the sounds of the forest as it settled into the coming night. The sun had gone down hours ago thanks to the mountains he called home, but true sunset still had a few minutes. He'd lived in Whispering Springs or the surrounding mountain range his whole life.

Never once had he felt the urge to leave it behind and explore the world. He took the occasional trip down the mountainside to visit one of the big cities, but there was no appeal in staying away longer than a day or two, a week at most.

He breathed deep, pulling the chilled, late-spring air into his lungs, the accompanying sting of cold meeting warm, a welcome twinge. His house had been finished for two months, but he hadn't moved everything in until this past weekend.

A grin curled his lips as he thought about why it had taken so long. Having his two best friends somewhat occupied with Rowan's return had slowed down both the finishing of the house and the moving in. Not that he'd complain. Steve was more than happy Rowan had finally come home and even happier to see her reunited with her mate, Quinn.

The night around him grew still, quiet in a way that pricked his instincts, caused his hair to stand on end, and drew his coyote's attention. Steve slowly sat forward, leaned over to put his beer bottle on the deck beside his chair, before closing his eyes and honing his senses to listen—to smell. The crush of undergrowth beneath running feet hit him first, followed by a body-slamming gust of fear. He scented two shifters but he couldn't place them. Tried harder to separate them and connect either essence to the memory of its owner.

A howl of agony echoed up the ridge, sliced into his gut and pulled his coyote out with amazing speed. On his feet, Steve was glad he'd forgone shirt and shoes after his shower as he removed his sweats. Free of the restrictive garment, he shifted as he leapt over the deck railing to the ground one story below. He landed with a jolt to every bone but ignored it as he ran through the forest in the direction of the horrific screams of distress.

As he drew closer he could hear the struggles, smell the fear—the blood. *The enjoyment.* The attacker, in coyote form if he wasn't mistaken, was thrilled with his catch. A catch Steve had every intention of setting free. His muscles shuddered and it wasn't just from the exertion of running all out. He thought about stealth but a bloodcurdling cry and bark of triumph changed his mind. Low branches and shrubs slapped into him, tangled with his fur, as he powered his bulk toward the fight up ahead he glimpsed through the trees.

The other animal's head whipped up, yellow eyes and white teeth glowed in the dusk as he turned in Steve's direction. A frustrated howl rent the air as the coyote turned from his prey and bolted in the opposite direction. Torn between going after the retreating coyote and tending to the victim, Steve hesitated enough to have the decision made for him. Whoever the coyote was, he had too much head start and the metallic stench of blood told Steve his first concern should be the wounded human crumpled on the ground.

Ripped, blood-splattered clothes covered the too-still body, but there was no mistaking the feminine shape or perfume. He reached her side and shifted back to human form. Uncaring of his naked state, he knelt beside her head and felt for a pulse. The steady beat reassured him but how long would it stay that way? The overpowering aroma of spilled blood masked her scent, but he knew she was one of the pack, her scent was familiar. Too familiar.

No!

His fingers trembled as he brushed away hair to reveal the face he saw in his dreams and Steve's heart stopped.

"Doc?" The hoarse whisper ached in his throat.

His heart kicked back in with a thud. Adrenaline pumped through his veins and the urge to cradle her in his arms took hold but Steve knew he couldn't. Not yet. He had to check her injuries, stop the bleeding if he could. He ran his hands down her limbs to check for broken bones. In his limited knowledge he held back a howl of frustration. She was the one who should be doing this. She was the doctor. The person who stitched the cuts, set the broken bones and soothed the bruises.

Hands and fingers sticky with blood, Steve rolled her to her back and breathed a sigh of relief when she moaned.

"Doc? Can you hear me?"

She shuddered under his touch but didn't answer as he tried to find where she bled from the most. Her jeans and shirt were wet with blood but he couldn't find anything too deep or gushing enough to take the time to stop the flow. He needed to get her to the house. There he could remove what was left of her clothes and see how bad the damage was under light. He could also clean her up and decide if she required medical attention better than he could give.

They were about three hundred feet below his house but with the slope and thick vegetation, that distance may as well be three miles. It would take him longer to get up the hill than it had coming down with the burden of carrying Doc, and Steve knew every second counted. He tried to be as gentle as possible, but she whimpered when he worked his arms under her and pulled her against his naked chest.

In all the fantasies he'd had of Doc cradled against his naked body, this wasn't one of them. The woman set his blood on fire but carrying her now froze that same blood in his veins. Knowing someone had set out to hurt her—*had hurt her*—made Steve's coyote want to hunt down her attacker and do some hurting of his own. He turned and headed for home, careful not to let any branches scrape against her battered body. By the time he reached halfway, shivers raked her from head to toe and he knew shock had set in.

He lengthened his stride. The urgency to get her home giving him the strength to move over the ground quickly. When the large, dark shadow of his house came into view he breathed a sigh of relief and went toward the basement door. Once inside, Steve did something he'd never done before. He closed the solid timber panel and threw the deadbolt home.

The house was dark—quiet, but he stopped to listen in case they weren't alone. There was nothing different from when he'd left. No new scents and Steve's instincts told him no one was inside—or had been. He took the stairs to the main floor, Doc held tight in his embrace. It never entered his mind to take her to a guest room. Instead he headed straight for his bedroom, laid her on his bed and switched the bedside light on to get his first good look at her.

Steve sucked in a breath. Her delicate face was bruised and

bloody, one eye swollen and the shiner already showing. The split in her bottom lip looked bad, it gaped open and blood flowed in a thin line down her chin. The dark shadow along the right side of her jaw worried him. She'd obviously taken one to the chin at some point, whether a direct strike or glancing blow he couldn't say. Doc reminded him of a prize fighter after ten rounds in the ring.

As gently as he could, he removed her clothes. He started at her feet, tossing her boots to the floor behind him. Her jeans were torn in places and the patches of blood, while concerning, didn't seem to be life threatening. Steve popped the button and tugged the zipper down. Lucky for him, Doc chose to wear clothes too big for her petite frame and the pants slid down over her hips with little resistance. With her legs bare he could see the scratches and knew the heavy denim had saved her from worse harm.

When only her bra and panties covered her, Steve ducked into his bathroom for the first-aid kit. He filled a small bowl with warm water and grabbed a washcloth and towel. The dirt and blood needed to be cleaned away before he could treat her wounds and assess the damage.

She hadn't moved or made more than the occasional whimper since they came inside and the worry of her lack of response played on Steve's mind. Should he have taken her straight to town? No point second-guessing now. He had to take care of her as best he could.

Most of the lacerations were minor except one across her left breast had him more than a little concerned. He had to remove her bra to see the entire wound. It went from the top curve below her collarbone to just under her nipple and the two shallow scratches either side of the deep cut told him a paw had caught the tender flesh and sliced it.

His back teeth would be ground to stumps by the time he

finished. The need to hunt down her attacker burned in his gut and his coyote yanked to be let free but Steve couldn't do anything yet. Doc needed him and he wouldn't go off and leave her. He couldn't no matter how much his animal side wanted to.

Doc whimpered and moaned while he cleaned the lesser scrapes but jerked awake as he swiped the large gash on her breast. Her body stiffened and he waited for the panic, for her to fight him but her instincts were good, she just opened the eye that wasn't swollen shut and watched him as he cleaned, then treated the wound with disinfectant lotion.

"You're safe now, Gordie, I won't let anyone hurt you again." His words did little to soothe his agitated nerves but she relaxed into the bed.

Steve rolled her to the side, took care of the cuts on her back before easing her over again. The marks on her face were the only ones left to deal with and he wasn't at all sure what to do about her lip, but first he'd get her one of his shirts. He didn't want her to get cold and he didn't think Doc would be too happy when she came to her senses a bit more and found herself all but naked in his bed.

He'd been trying to get her there for years but no matter what he did, Steve could never convince her that's where she belonged. Having her here now, like this, tore him up inside.

He had what he'd always wanted but at what cost?

GORDIE WATCHED STEVE. The barest of tremors shook his hands as he tended to her injuries. Her focus was off, one eye blurry and the other refused to open. Dizziness made her nauseated and the churning of her stomach warned of possible rebellion. Taking slow, deep breaths she catalogued the damage. Nothing felt broken, but she was pretty sure she had a mild concussion.

She hadn't seen it coming. One second she was walking through the forest and the next she received a punch in the face. The blow snapped her head back and slammed her into a tree. For a moment Gordie was stunned, and her attacker managed a few more good hits before shock wore off and she began to fight back. A kick to the balls had given her precious seconds to run. She hadn't counted on him shifting.

Fear sliced through Gordie as Steve stood.

"Don't leave me." The words came out garbled and the pain that lanced her lip made her cry out.

"Easy. I'm not going anywhere." He was back beside her, brushing her cheek with his fingertips. "I'm just getting a shirt for you to put on."

She squeezed her eye shut and breathed deep. Pain radiated out through her chest, the side she'd landed on when the coyote had pounced on her burned and Gordie knew the fact she was bruised and not broken was a miracle. The sting of tears scalded her eyes and scratched the back of her throat. She wouldn't cry. *She wouldn't.*

Gordie tried to swallow but her mouth was dry. Her tongue slid out to lick her lip and she jerked on the bed, the pain excruciating, and an agonized shriek left her throat.

"Easy, baby." Warm hands soothed her, skirting around the numerous aches. "Let's get you covered up so I can take a look at that mouth."

Her body vibrated with the strain of holding the sobs at bay. The bed lifted and Steve's warmth disappeared. Suddenly cold, Gordie shivered, the quaking built in intensity until her teeth chattered. When the mattress dipped and heat brushed against her hip, Gordie shook so violently every part of her screamed in pain.

Groaning, she turned into him as he leaned over to help her sit. With gentleness she'd never expected, Steve tugged a soft flannel shirt up her arm and around her back.

It proved more difficult to get her second arm into the sleeve. Whimpers and moans filled the air. Muscles tense with pain refused to cooperate and Gordie could do little to help. With her arm in at last, Steve lowered her to the bed. Her back spasmed, agony speared up her spine to throb painfully at the base of her skull. Her head swam and her stomach churned. Bile rose in her throat and she turned to the side.

Either Steve had worked out what was about to happen or the man had lightning-fast reflexes. He had the wastepaper basket under her face as she leaned over the edge of the mattress. Abdominal muscles contracted, repelling everything in her stomach up her throat. Acid burned and the metallic taste of blood filled her mouth, making her heave harder. Sweat popped out on her skin, and goose bumps followed by uncontrollable shaking rode alongside the piercing pain of her twisted belly.

He held her hair out of the way, his other hand holding the bin while she emptied the contents of her stomach. Tears streamed down her face and mucus ran from her nose. As the convulsions eased, Gordie slumped forward in exhaustion. The pain receded, her body going numb, and the effort to stay awake grew more difficult. Steve moved her back from the edge, used a pillow to prop her up. Her head drooped and Gordie knew she would be out in seconds but she needed to make something clear first.

"No hospital." Her lip stung and hot fluid trickled down her chin.

"Shit, Doc. I can't stitch that lip and it needs a few. I need to get you to someone who can take care of it."

"No. Hospital." Her words slurred as blackness closed in.

"Gordie."

"Please." The word came out a sob.

"Okay."

"Promise me." She couldn't leave Whispering Springs and she was the only medical personnel on the mountain. She just needed to rest and then she'd be okay to stitch the wound herself.

Steve must have leaned over her because warm, mint-fresh breath fanned out across her face as he sighed. "Okay, Gordie. I promise."

His fingers brushed away the strands of hair stuck to her forehead, his gentle touch again surprising her. Steve was a large man, one she usually avoided touching but not through fear of physical harm. No, he scared her for other reasons she chose to ignore. But as drowsiness pulled at her, the last thing to play across her mind was the big man who treated her with such care.

STEVE CURSED himself a fool as he cleaned Doc's face. He'd given his word and he wouldn't go back on it, but damn, she needed to have her lip tended to. He could stitch it but he knew there would be a horrible scar if he tried. She'd heal quickly with her coyote DNA, but without stitches it would leave her with a visible reminder. The bruising on her face had already gone a deep blue-black, moving through the phases of healing quickly.

The blood and dirt were gone but he hadn't used the disinfectant yet. He wanted to keep his promise but he also needed to know she was okay and he didn't think he possessed enough skill to trust his own judgment. Blowing out a breath, he rummaged through the first-aid kit, hoping to find something that would pull the two sides of her lip together and hold them there. His fingers landed on a box of steri-strips and he ripped it open to examine the small bandages.

They could work. Doc would need to keep her mouth still and he'd have to watch the wound for infection, but if he used a couple of the strips to pull the sections of lip together it would hold and allow her body to heal. Reading the instructions one more time, Steve laid everything out within easy reach. Once he had the area clean and dry, he pushed the open sides of the cut together and stuck a strip on.

Three more and he'd done the best job he could. He sat back to admire his handiwork and laughed ruefully. Not the best-looking bandage he'd ever seen but it would do for now.

He gathered up the discarded wrappers and went to throw them into the waste bin next to the bed but remembered just in time he'd used it to catch her vomit. Putting them in a pile beside him, he pulled the first-aid kit back together and returned it to the bathroom where he tossed the garbage in the bin.

Back in his room, he cleared away Doc's bloody clothes, the waste basket and the bowl of now-cold water. Steve made sure she was resting before he went to get his pants from the back deck. Detouring past the front door, he locked it. No way would he allow anyone the chance to get near Doc again.

His pants and beer retrieved, he locked the sliding door to the deck and went to the kitchen. He dumped the untouched warm beer down the sink before he threw the bottle in the bin. Forgoing another one, he grabbed a soda instead. He'd need his wits about him from now on.

Not that one beer would get him drunk, but anything that slowed his reflexes was off his agenda until he found the bastard responsible for Doc's attack. Throwing his pants in the laundry as he walked by, Steve made his way back to the bedroom. Happy to see Doc resting easy, he slipped into the bathroom for a quick shower.

With a twist of a tap had the water running. He swallowed the last of the soda and dropped the can in the bin before stepping into the glass enclosure. Water flowed down his body and he tilted his face into the spray to let the hot stream wash the dirt and sweat—the blood from his chest—away.

A shudder traveled through him. The thought of Doc's spilled blood made his own boil with anger and the urge to hunt and destroy the person who'd hurt her. His jaw clenched and he ground his molars hard. They'd pay for touching her, but he needed to focus on Doc before he could take revenge.

Steve soaped himself and rinsed. For the second time tonight, he shut the shower off and stepped out. Brisk movements dragged the towel over his skin, soaking up the moisture and abrading nerve endings already on edge. He tucked the towel over the rail and ran his fingers through his wet hair. Emotions bombarded him. He wanted to hold Doc close and keep her safe but he also wanted to go out and hunt down her attacker.

Frustration tore at him, but Steve knew the only thing he'd be doing tonight would be watching over Doc. He gave himself a shake to loosen his tense muscles before he left the bathroom and returned to Gordie. The scent of blood still tainted the air and his jaw clenched with renewed anger. Pausing, he made a conscious effort to relax. It wouldn't do her any good to feel his rage and for now it had to be all about Doc.

Making his way to the chest of drawers, he pulled out a pair of boxers and stepped into them. Three strides had him beside the bed. Doc was on top of the bedcovers but he didn't want to disturb her so he pulled a blanket from the back of his cupboard and draped it over her. Walking to the other side of the bed he lifted the edge of the cover and crawled in next to her.

He wanted to pull her into his arms but he didn't think he could without hurting her and the last thing he wanted was to add to her pain. Steve reached over to the bedside lamp and switched it off. Moonlight streamed through the window and skylight, bathing the room in a soft glow. Doc lay on her side, facing him, her body curled up as though protecting herself from further harm. His heart ached at how vulnerable she appeared.

Resistance was futile. The woman he wanted to the depth of his soul lay hurting alongside him and he had to touch her. With the tip of one finger he brushed the hair from her eyes. She moved into his caress and he couldn't stop the smile that pulled at his mouth. In her most unguarded moment, she knew him, reached for him. Her actions contradicting every protest she'd made about their attraction.

For three years he'd respected her need to push him away. He knew her denial of their attraction stemmed from the trauma of losing her husband and unborn child, but enough was enough. From now on she wouldn't keep him at arm's length. He'd make sure of it. It was time for her to accept him as her mate. She could object all she wanted, but Steve wasn't about to let things continue the way they had been.

Not after tonight.

He understood her need to protect herself but in doing so she was denying both of them happiness. The fear of being mated had stopped him from pursuing her when they were teenagers, that and her being human. It had terrified him back then and by the time he'd gotten his head around it Anthony had stolen her out from under his nose. Steve didn't plan on letting that happen again and he'd be damned if he would let her fight him any longer.

It was time to claim what was his.

GORDIE'S first registered thought was pain. Everything hurt. From the tips of her toes to the top of her head, every cell screamed in agony—even her eyelashes as they weighed down her lids. She tried not to move, tried to keep her breathing shallow to stop the vise from crushing her chest. The second thing Gordie registered was the warm body she'd curled herself around. A steady heartbeat drummed beneath the hot flesh pressed to her face. Confusion filled her. Where was she? And who was in her bed?

"Easy, Doc. It's just me." The muscles beneath her cheek vibrated as Steve's voice rumbled through his chest and filled her ears.

The urge to pull away took hold but the slightest movement brought pain. Gordie opened her eyes, one barely more than a crack, and stared at the hard male chest before her. Bits and pieces of the night before started to flit through her mind and she groaned. The walk she'd taken after dinner, the need to be near Steve but not near him.

The attack.

Steve's arms loosened, giving her the freedom to move away if she wanted. But for the first time in three years Gordie wanted to be close to him. She needed him to hold her, to remind her she was alive—safe.

"Do you feel up to talking about what happened?"

Not wanting the ugliness of the night before intruding on the moment, she shook her head. Pain ricocheted around her skull, making her groan.

He didn't comment, just tightened his arms again and pulled her a little closer to his side. Warmth and rightness invaded her. The truth of what she'd been denying since her return to Whispering Springs and the mountains that had been her home from the age of six, slammed into her like never before. It terrified her like never before too, but she couldn't pull away from him. Not after last night. She felt vulnerable—scared, and Steve's steady presence reassured her.

They lay quietly in the predawn light. For long moments Gordie just enjoyed the safety and comfort Steve offered. She knew she'd have to go soon enough, knew she needed to check her wounds and return home. But she didn't want to leave his warm embrace. Wanted to stay wrapped in his arms and let him hold her and make everything disappear. But she couldn't expect Steve to take care of her problems for her.

Before last night Gordie hadn't been too concerned by the strange little things that had occurred over the last month. Random things moved at both her house and the clinic. Doors unlocked when she would swear she'd locked them. The creepy, itchy-neck feeling of being watched all the time. None of it had worried her because she'd been so busy she could have forgotten she'd moved that picture or those supplies—or even neglected to lock up after herself.

She couldn't ignore them anymore.

But she dare not tell anyone either. She had no real evidence and nothing but the gut-gnawing instinct that Marcus was behind what had been happening. The only proof anything was actually going on was last night's attack and she hadn't gotten a clear look at her assailant.

She wasn't even sure she'd identified his scent correctly. Even after all the years as a coyote shifter she still couldn't use her senses well. Maybe if she hadn't tried to ignore her wild side she might have had better luck.

Gordie had spent the years since Anthony's death denying her coyote existed whenever possible. She shifted when the pull became too much but other than that, her animal lay slumbering. Unless Steve was around—which was the reason she kept her distance from him. When he was near, her coyote sat up and took notice, wanted to break free and run wild to be with the animal she recognized as her mate. In the last few months staying away from him had become more difficult.

Her need to be close to him had driven her to take walks in the forest below his new home. Before he'd moved into his mountain house they'd lived on the same street and it wasn't until he'd started staying up on the mountain overnight that her true needs had shown themselves.

She'd managed to delude herself for so long. Believed she had her feelings under control. The wild rush of urges and desires had never been a part of her life before. She'd never felt this drawn to Anthony.

Even after he'd turned her, Anthony didn't make her pulse race or her coyote pull to be free. The guilt she'd lived with for years still haunted her. Gordie had hurt Anthony by accepting his love when she hadn't loved him in return. Not the way she should have—the way he deserved.

He'd been her friend and she'd been so desperate to become like everyone else in Whispering Springs she'd gladly taken all he offered. They'd both paid dearly for her mistake. She'd spent the years since his death trying to make up for her decision but the guilt remained.

Gordie closed her eyes tight. Tried to stop her brain from taking her into that dark place she'd locked away the day she left Whispering Springs to attend college. Now was not the time to dwell on the past. She had to think about what to do in the present. Because if she was right in her assumption of who had started a campaign of terror against her, she was in a whole heap of trouble and so was the rest of the pack.

～

DOC WAS OVERTHINKING AGAIN. The woman had a brain that wouldn't quit. While that was good when she was in her doctor role, Steve wished she'd let it rest and just feel for once. Then she might see how right it was for them to be together.

He'd let her push him away, let her rationalize until they were both blue in the face but he wouldn't give her that luxury anymore. From now on they were a couple. He wouldn't push her to mate but in every other area she'd have to accept him by her side.

First he needed to check her wounds and decide whether she should see someone about her lip. He'd dozed on and off since he'd crawled into bed, so he knew Doc had spent a restless night beside him. After he took care of her injuries he'd make them both something to eat, the healing process would require extra nourishment and he planned to make sure she got it. Then they'd talk and she could answer some questions, like what she was doing this far out of town in the forest after dark. Alone.

"I need to have a look at your injuries. I'm not sure I did a good job with your lip but I'm not the doctor here." Steve eased her face up with two fingers under her chin.

He gently cradled her cheek in his palm. The gash looked to be knitting together already. That and the bruising along her jaw and around her eyes made his stomach churn and his coyote wanted to rip apart the person responsible for the damage. It took effort and a bit more enamel ground from his back teeth but he managed to not squeeze her face in his frustration and anger. Steve let his fingertips trail the dark bruise along Doc's chin, the petite angle of her face marred by the ugly mark.

"Damn, Doc. You really got yourself done over. Wanna tell me what happened?"

She stiffened in his arms and fear flashed in her gaze before she looked away. Either she'd been more than physically hurt in the attack or she was attempting to shut him out again.

"Don't try to shut me out. I'm finished with you pushing me away. Dancing around what we are, ends now, Doc." He placed a kiss on top of her head. "I'll wait on the mating, I won't push you on being physically intimate, but I will push you on everything else. From now on we're together whether we have sex or not."

He held her close, rubbed his hand up and down her back until she relaxed against him once more.

"You can't fight what we are forever, Doc. I understand your fear and I'll be patient as best I can but you have to know our mating is inevitable. Neither of us is strong enough to fight these feelings forever."

Warm air whispered over his chest, ruffling his hair and bathing his nipple in a wave of moist heat. Her breasts, concealed by his shirt, pressed into his side as she sucked in a deep breath, their taut peaks poking into his ribcage. The sensations of holding Doc so close bombarded him and his body reacted in typical male fashion. His pulse raced and blood pumped into his cock. He ignored his coyote's call to claim his mate and just held her. She remained quiet for so long Steve thought she would continue to deny their connection but she surprised him.

"I know I can't fight it anymore. I realized that when you moved up here but I'm not ready to take the next step." Her words were barely a murmur but he heard every one as if it were a physical blow to his heart.

"We'll worry about that later. Right now, let's get you all fixed up." Steve gently eased Doc away and turned her onto her back. He leaned up on his elbow and studied her face. "You know, you don't look as bad as I thought you would this morning."

The corners of her mouth tipped up and she winced. "Shoot, that hurt."

"Yeah, your lip is split down the middle. Try not to move your mouth."

"Talking isn't that bad because I can do it without moving my lips too much but smiling is obviously out of the question." She brought her hand up and ran her fingertips over his make-do bandage job.

Steve frowned. "It's not the most professional job, but working with what I have on hand and you extracting that promise you got the best I could offer."

"It feels okay but I should check it."

Doc tried to sit up but he stopped her with a hand on her shoulder. "Stay there. I'll grab the first-aid kit and a mirror." He rolled off the bed and walked around to her side. "Here, let me help you sit."

He pulled the pillows from his side of the bed and, easing her forward, stacked them behind her. Doc closed her eyes as she leaned back. "Do you have any pain pills?"

"Yeah. I'll bring everything I've got." He strode from the room and into his bathroom.

It didn't take long to pull out his supplies, he wasn't exactly overflowing with medical paraphernalia. Steve brought back his haul and dropped it on the bed beside Doc. He walked to his dresser and pulled his mother's hand mirror from the top drawer and headed back to Doc to find her going through his kit.

"This is all you have?"

It was a simple question but there was so much censure in those five words. Sheepishly he said, "Sorry, I'm not as familiar with all this stuff as you are."

Doc looked up, their gazes colliding. "Remind me to make you up a kit, these store-bought jobs are okay but I can give you a better one from the clinic." She barely moved her lips when she spoke but her words were clear.

Steve watched as Doc pulled out bandages, scissors and tape. She held the box of steri-strips before discarding them and searching the small plastic tub for something else. A breath huffed through her nose as she stopped combing the contents and went back to the packet of strips.

"You don't have sutures?"

He shook his head. "No. Only what came in the kit."

She sighed and picked up his mother's mirror. Her eyes widened when she saw her beaten-up face for the first time. The fingers she brought up to brush over the bandage on her lip trembled and her brown eyes filled with moisture. "Damn."

"Yeah, it's not pretty but it's already started to heal."

Doc brushed her fingertips along the bruise on her jaw. "This was the first punch," she murmured.

Steve's gut knotted and his coyote snarled. He managed to keep from voicing his rage. "What were you doing out in the woods?"

Her gaze met his, the dark depths held so much churning emotion the knot in his stomach tightened. "I wanted to be near you."

"You were in the forest to be near me?" He didn't understand how that was near him at all. Why hadn't she just knocked on his door?

"Ever since you moved up here I've been walking in the woods to be close. I needed to feel you."

"Jesus, Doc, you're killing me here." He reached out, ran his fingers down her cheek. "No more. You want to feel me, you come inside."

She turned away and Steve put gentle pressure on her chin

to make her look at him. "Promise me, Gordie. I don't want you going anywhere alone again."

His heart stalled while he waited for her answer. When she nodded he released the breath he held and leaned forward. As lightly as he could, Steve pressed his lips to hers. He stilled, savored the heat and feel of her mouth against his. The urge for more rolled over him and he groaned. Before he could take what he so desperately wanted he pulled back and rested his forehead on hers.

"Okay." He breathed deep. "Let's get you fixed up to your standards."

Doc didn't speak while he helped her remove the bandage from her mouth. The wound, like the rest of her injuries, had begun to heal. He held the strips ready for her to apply and by the time she'd finished he was more ashamed of the crappy job he'd done the night before.

"It's not so bad. I doubt I could have done a better job earlier, not without sutures." Her words, he knew, were supposed to reassure him but nothing except an uninjured Doc could do that.

"Feel like eating?" Steve gathered up what was left of the first-aid kit and the trash. "You need to build up your strength. I'm no chef, but I can open a can of soup."

"I'm not sure my stomach is up to eating yet, but you're right. And a bowl of warm soup sounds wonderful." The smile in her voice didn't move her lips or reach her eyes but that wasn't surprising when she had to still be in pain.

"I'll grab those pain pills and a glass of water first." He stood and turned for the door but Doc's voice stopped him before he took a step.

"Steve?"

He turned to face her. "What do you need?"

"Thank you." Her mouth curled slightly on the ends and she couldn't hide the flinch the action caused. "For everything."

Steve sighed. "Gordie you know I'd do anything you asked. The trouble is, until last night you never needed me." He spun around and strode from the room. Emotions collided inside him. Love, desire, rejection, guilt, frustration. One thing about Doc, she made him feel it all.

GORDIE SANK into the soft pillows at her back and closed her eyes. She'd swallowed the pain meds under Steve's watchful eye before he'd gone to the kitchen to heat some soup. It wasn't exactly a nutritional breakfast but at the moment that was the least of her concerns. She needed food while she healed—any food. Her aches had lessened since she'd woken, whether that was the pills starting to work or her own body healing she couldn't say, and really didn't care.

She couldn't bring herself to care about much of anything right now. Having Steve look after her, tending her injuries with such a gentle touch had soothed her in a way she hadn't expected. As much as she'd told him she wasn't ready for the next step in their relationship, Gordie couldn't deny she was closer than ever to giving in to her need for him. The edge of fear that always accompanied her emotions when she thought of Steve and what they could be had disappeared in the space of a few hours.

For years she'd used that fear to keep her distance. Without it, Gordie knew it was only a matter of time before they took the final step. Only one thing stood between them now. She needed to make peace with her past and the guilt she'd lived with for so long. Anthony would be the first person to encourage her to move on, but he wasn't here to nag her into it and as much as it hadn't been on a soul-deep level, she *had* loved him, still mourned his loss as though it happened yesterday.

Letting go of her guilt would be like losing Anthony all over again but it wouldn't be fair to Steve or her to take their attraction further until she had. The attack last night only served to remind her that life was short, too short to not take the happiness offered. Gordie hoped Steve had meant what he said about no pressure. With everything going on in her life right now she didn't think they'd be taking that final step anytime soon.

2

DECEMBER TWENTY-THIRD

STEVE'S BOOTS crunched through the fresh layer of snow on the ground as he made his way to the back door. Knocking the slush from his heels, he slipped through the open door and shut it behind him, making sure the deadlock engaged. His gut tightened. It wasn't like Doc to leave the clinic open after hours.

Careful not to make a sound, he turned and listened. Various motors associated with a doctor's office hummed and the tick of a clock beat steadily but Steve couldn't detect any other noise.

Where was Doc? Steve hadn't seen her outside when he pulled up and he'd driven past the front of the building on his way to the back alley. She was expecting him. They'd spoken on the phone not fifteen minutes earlier. So where the hell was she and why was the clinic left unlocked?

Something was wrong. Had been for weeks but Doc refused to talk about it. He cursed her for keeping him at arm's length. Still.

His senses were on full alert as he stepped along the dark

corridor. The door to Doc's office was wide open, the chair pushed back from the desk as though she'd gotten up in a hurry. A chill slid down Steve's spine and the hair across his nape stood on end. He went deeper into the building. The next door was closed and he placed his ear against the timber. No sound came from the other side, not that he expected to hear anyone in the storeroom.

Doc kept the room locked unless she was in there but he tried the knob regardless. It didn't budge. Noise farther down the hall had his head snapping around. There was no one in sight and the place had gone quiet as a tomb again but he'd definitely heard something.

Gordie, where the hell are you?

The next room he came to served as the theater and morgue. Steve peered around the door frame. At a glance everything appeared to be in place so he moved on to the first examination room. Bright murals and mobiles made the children's exam room like a playground and other than the gentle sway of the coyotes dangling from the ceiling where the central heating duct blew warm air into the room, there was no movement.

Steve paused, listening for any sign of life. There were two more rooms plus the reception office and waiting area to search. His senses told him he wouldn't find anyone. He could smell Doc's lingering scent, but couldn't tell if she was here or not, the smells associated with any medical facility masked others and that made his instincts howl with frustration. She would never leave the clinic unattended and she certainly wouldn't leave the back door unlocked, never mind open.

He wanted to race through the rest of the building, throwing open doors and yelling Doc's name, but he stayed on the side of caution just in case he'd misjudged the situation. What danger could be lurking he hadn't a clue and he didn't really want to find out. All he wanted was Gordie. To know she was safe. He stepped into the next exam room. Movement to the left in his peripheral vision made him turn and crouch.

A large, silver blur rushed past his temple, ruffling his hair and almost making him miss the other, smaller steel implements flying in his direction. He ducked and rolled to the side. Landing on his stomach, he looked across the room. Gordie stood with her arms raised, an instrument tray in her hands, and the look of fear on her face brought his protective instincts and coyote screaming to the surface. Steve barely held on to his human side. Something or someone had terrified his mate and he was ready and willing to take that threat apart.

"Gordie!" Steve remained still, strained against the need to go to her, and tried to show the frightened woman he wasn't a danger. "It's me. Steve."

Her face drained of color and her shoulders sagged as she lowered the tray. "Oh God. Steve?" Her words were no more than a breath.

"Yeah, baby, it's me." He slowly pushed off the floor. "The door was open, Doc."

"The door?" Her gaze darted to the doorway behind him.

Her vagueness worried him. Whatever had caused her fear had done a real number on her. She hadn't been this shaken up after the brutal attack months ago. He took a step toward her, his movement made her flinch, the metal tray dropping to the floor at her feet with a spine-rattling crash. Doc's hands clenched into fists at her sides but the action didn't hide the fact she was trembling.

He took another step, kept the motion smooth so as not to startle her again. Steve quickened his pace when she swayed. He'd taken two strides when she began to crumple to the floor. Darting forward, he barely caught her in time and he ended up sitting on the cold linoleum, Doc cradled in his lap. She threw her arms around his neck, buried her face against his chest and burst into tears.

Dumbstruck by this vulnerable Doc in his arms, it took Steve a moment to think straight. Holding her close, he rocked them, ran his hands up and down her back, and whispered words of reassurance he wasn't even sure he believed. He told her it would be all right but he had no idea if his words were true when he had no clue about what had happened.

When her sobbing eased off to the odd hiccup, Steve reached into his pocket for his phone. It took him a couple of tries but he finally got the number he was after and hit call. He listened to two rings before a deep voice answered.

"Dale Turner."

"Come to the clinic."

"What the hell is going on, McKenna?"

"I don't know exactly but you need to come now."

"I'll be there in five."

The line went dead in his ear. He pulled the phone back into view and scrolled through his address book. Hitting call a second time, Steve brought the device back to his ear. It rang five times before Brogan picked up.

"Wilder."

"Where are you?"

"In town, why?"

"You need to come to the clinic."

"I'm not liking the sound of your voice, Steve."

"Neither am I but I'm dealing. Just get here." He hung up before his friend could question him further.

Pocketing the phone, he shifted Doc so he could get them off the floor. She lay limp in his arms as he got to his feet and walked over to the exam table. Placing her on the bed proved difficult when she wouldn't let go of his neck.

"I'm not leaving but I have to let the sheriff in when he gets here." Loud banging echoed down the hallway. "That'll be him now. I'm coming right back."

Steve untangled her arms and settled her back on the pillow. He grabbed the folded blanket from the foot rail, shook it out and spread it over her, tucking in the sides. He brushed a hand over her face, pushing her hair out of her eyes. "Be right back."

Making his way to reception at a jog, he crossed the waiting area and unlocked the front door. Dale, Brogan and Quinn charged in, making Steve jump back or be knocked down by the three men. He started to shut the door when Rowan and El stepped inside.

"Well, the gang's all here."

"Cut the crap, McKenna. What the fuck's going on?" Brogan demanded.

Steve sighed. "I don't know exactly yet. I got here about ten minutes ago and the back door was open with no one in sight."

"Where was Gordie?" Rowan asked.

"In the exam room but I didn't know that then."

"What do you mean by that?" Dale stepped closer.

"I'll explain everything but first I have to get back to Doc." Steve turned, throwing over his shoulder, "Make sure you secure the door."

"Secure the door? Just what the fuck is going on, Steve?" Brogan boomed.

"Stop yelling. Doc's nerves are frayed enough without you adding to it." Steve entered the exam room to find Gordie had turned on her side facing the doorway. Her eyes where huge in her chalk-white face and his gut knotted. He walked over and gathered her into his arms, needing to feel her against him to know she was safe.

Wrapped in the blanket, she curled up on his lap as he took a seat in a chair. She trembled and in spite of the blanket and warm room, her body temperature had gone down as though she'd been outside without her coat.

"Gordie?" Rowan knelt at his feet, brushed her hand over Gordie's head. "Can I get you something? A drink maybe?"

"Tea. Warm, sweet tea will help." El patted Doc's shoulder. "I'll get a cup."

Steve loved that their group of friends were rallying around Doc but hated that she needed them at all. He'd give her another minute to warm up before he asked any questions. The three men stood in the room like a barricade against any further threat, their menacing faces enough to scare off the toughest of adversaries, known or otherwise.

El returned with a mug of tea and Steve held it to Doc's lips. She sipped, her hands wrapping around the cup and his hand. Her fingers interlocked with his and she gave him a gentle squeeze before she pushed the hot drink away and sat up.

"I'm okay." She sighed before lowering her head to rest on his shoulder.

"Wanna tell us what happened?" Steve asked.

"Not really much to tell. Someone was in the clinic. I'd locked up before talking to you so I don't know how they got in. Or how they got out."

"Out's easy. They went through the back door. It was open when I got here." He handed the mug to Rowan. "Did you get a look at who it was? Were they after drugs?"

Doc let out a chest-shaking sigh. "This is going to sound stupid and I won't blame any of you for thinking me crazy."

Dale laughed. "You're the least crazy person on the planet, Doc."

"Besides, in the last year there's been lots of crazy shit going on in this town," Brogan added.

"He was in black from head to foot. A beanie on his head

and some sort of scarf over his face but I'd know those eyes anywhere."

Steve tensed. He knew what was coming, felt it in his bones and yet it still hit him like a two-by-four when Doc said the name.

"Marcus." She shuddered and sagged against him. "It was Marcus."

"Son of a bitch." Brogan lunged for El as she slumped to the floor. "Shit."

"I'm okay, Brogan. A little wobbly in the knees, but I'm okay," El said.

"Jesus, woman. Don't *do* that." Brogan held her in his arms.

Steve almost laughed at the terrified tone in his friend's voice but he knew all too well what Marcus was capable of doing. It had only been a few weeks since the maniac had had El at his mercy so her weak knees were understandable.

"Are you sure, Doc?" Dale asked.

"She wouldn't have said it if she wasn't," Steve snapped.

"Whoa." Dale held up his hands. "Just checking. It's my job, remember?"

Steve relaxed his tight grip on Gordie. "Sorry, but Doc doesn't lie."

"Never said she did but adrenaline can do a number on you and so can fear. She wouldn't be the first victim to make a mistake."

"No mistake." Gordie shifted in Steve's arms. "Help me sit up, Steve. It's time we told everyone about last May."

"While you're at it maybe you'll tell us what's been going on for weeks now too?" Steve was over being kept in the dark. If Doc was prepared to reveal what had happened back in spring then she could damn well tell him what the fuck had been going on recently.

~

GORDIE KNEW STEVE WAS RIGHT. She hadn't mentioned any of the events leading up to last May's attack or the ones in recent weeks to anyone but today showed her she couldn't deal with Marcus on her own. And there was no doubt in her mind that Marcus was behind everything. A shiver rippled through her. He'd gotten way too close this evening. He wouldn't get a second chance.

"Can we do this back at the house?" She looked at Steve. "I'd prefer to leave here. I'm not avoiding, putting off maybe, but I will tell you everything."

"I don't see why not. Any objections?" Dale asked.

"Yeah, I've got one." Steve's voice cut into her nerves and skated over her skin like ice. "You're not going back to your house."

"What? Of course I am. Where else would I go?"

"My place."

Gordie opened her mouth but didn't get out a sound, never mind a word.

"No arguments, Gordie. I'm done. No more running. No more hiding." His gaze bore into hers, slicing right to her soul. "Understand?"

There was no argument she could put forward. Not with every part of her shrieking for him to stay with her—hold her. In the months since that horrible night in the forest behind his house she'd made every excuse under the sun to keep him at arm's length. He'd pushed but he'd never once stepped over the invisible line she'd drawn between them. Until now.

She nodded.

It surprised Gordie, the relief that washed over her. She would have thought having Steve make the decision would chafe at her independent nature but it felt liberating—right.

They stared at each other, testing the new agreement between them. Steve broke the connection and turned to face the others.

"Rowan, can you go over to The Den and ask Kat for some of her famous beef stew to go? Oh, and you better see if she can come out to the house for this too. If not, tell her to come out when she's done for the night." Steve took charge with ease. "Quinn, can I get you to change the locks on the clinic? I'd do it but I want to get Doc home and comfortable before we hash through everything. I have a feeling this is going to take a while."

"Sure thing, I'll meet you out at your place. Brogan, you and El take Rowan with you."

"Gordie, do you want me to ask Kat to get you anything from your place?" Rowan asked.

"We'll deal with that tomorrow. She can make do with what she's got. The clinic is closed now through to New Year so Doc won't need anything in a hurry." Steve finally turned back to her. "Where's your purse?"

"In my office, bottom desk drawer." She still hadn't faced the room but she could hear shuffling and footsteps on the linoleum floor as her friends began to leave.

"Did you walk to work today? Your car wasn't out back," Steve asked.

"No, Kat brought me in. She stayed over last night." Gordie didn't tell him why she'd convinced her sister to spend the night. There was no point starting that conversation yet.

"Okay, let's go." Steve, still holding her in his arms, cradled her close and got to his feet. "Dale, are you following us out to the house now?"

"No, if it's all right with Doc, I'll wait for Quinn to get back with those locks and have a look around in the meantime."

"Do you think you'll find anything?" She tilted her head to look at Dale. "I mean, I didn't hear anything until he was right behind me, no doors opening, no footsteps, nothing." She shivered at the memory of turning around and coming face-to-face with Marcus.

"He's gone, Doc." Steve's quiet words, murmured in her ear, caused her tense muscles to relax. How he knew what she was thinking, Gordie couldn't begin to explain, and held in his warm embrace she didn't bother trying. She just snuggled closer.

In no time she found herself strapped into the front seat of Steve's pickup. The cab still had that new-car smell even though it was almost a year since he'd had to replace the vehicle. Gordie pushed away the memories of him using himself and his car as a barricade between Quinn and a madman. Brogan was right. In the last year Whispering Springs had seen more than its fair share of crazy.

They spent the drive out of town in silence. Gordie didn't mind. It gave her a few minutes to compose herself as the knowledge of what they'd be before this day was over began to sink in. This time the shiver that rolled down her spine had nothing to do with fear.

The thought of finally touching Steve like she'd wanted to for so long sent heat shooting through her veins to pool in delicate flesh. Her breasts felt heavy, her sex swollen. Moisture soaked her panties and she had to admit, if only to herself, he made her want things she'd never imagined.

Steve pulled into his attached garage and switched off the engine. The silence seemed to echo around them, the air vibrating with the stillness and Gordie quivered as the power of the moment flowed over her. Once they stepped from the car nothing would be the same.

No, the change had happened back at the clinic. When she'd needed Steve with a bone-deep ache that she'd registered even while consumed with fear. It was that one instant in time where the world had clicked into place and she'd seen the future as it should be. In a second she'd gone from terrified and panicked to calm and centered. She knew what she had to do. Survive at any cost.

Steve turned toward her, his forearm resting on the top of the steering wheel. He didn't speak, just watched her with that penetrating gaze. The one that read all her innermost thoughts and made her feel all squirmy inside. No man had ever affected her the way he did and until today Gordie hadn't thought herself capable of handling him. Now she knew differently.

"There's no turning back now, Doc." His fingers toyed with the ends of her hair.

She swallowed over the lump in her throat. "I know."

He smiled. "That easy?"

"It's amazing what a little fright can do for the senses." She tried to return his smile but it somehow slipped from her lips before it could form.

"Come here." Steve released her seatbelt and pulled her into his lap, pinning her between his body and the wheel. "You're safe here, Doc."

Gordie figured he meant in his house, but for her, safety was his arms, the security of his embrace and the strength he offered her willingly. She moved closer, nuzzled her face against the warmth of his neck and drew in his scent. It amazed her how just that small action could soothe her nerves and rile them at the same time.

"Gordie." Warm air ruffled her hair before she felt his lips press to her temple. "Come on, let's get inside or everyone will arrive and find us fucking in my truck."

She gasped. His use of strong language didn't bother her, it was the images the words provoked that made her breathless.

"Yeah, I'm that close." He chuckled as he opened the door and maneuvered them out of the cab.

"I can walk."

"I know, but I want to carry you and you're going to let me." His arms tightened around her.

"Okay."

Steve laughed. "All this easy agreement is starting to worry me, Doc."

"Don't worry. I'll be back to my disagreeable self soon enough and then you'll wish you hadn't started this."

"Never."

"You say that now..."

He swung her legs down until her toes barely touched the ground and pressed her against the side of his truck. "I'll say it forever."

She stared into his dark eyes and felt the truth of his words to the depth of her soul. Gordie watched as Steve lowered his head, his lips drawing closer to hers. His breath brushed over her skin in a butter-soft caress, a whisper of contact, a prelude of what would follow. From one heartbeat to the next his mouth was on hers, his tongue thrusting between her lips to delve inside.

Steve stroked his tongue over hers, toyed with her, coaxed her into joining him in his demand for more. She wound her arms around his neck and her legs around his waist, held on to him as hot lashes of lust struck her. Gordie pressed her body to his, crushed her breasts to his chest and ground her clit on the erection trapped between them. Pounding need thumped a beat as old as time as their mouths continued to devour.

On the verge of an orgasm, Gordie whimpered, the small sound swallowed as he drove the kiss deeper. His hands gripped her hips, pulling her tighter against his straining flesh and pressing into her clit with the perfect amount of pressure to send her into orbit. Convulsion after convulsion seized her.

Moisture flooded her panties and the aroma of her arousal floated around them.

He eased back, lightened the strokes of his tongue, and slowed the thrust of his hips. As the final waves of her climax ebbed away he pulled his mouth from hers. Breathing hard, Steve tucked her head under his chin and held her. Gordie struggled to catch her breath and her heart beat hard enough to bruise her ribs.

"I think we should take this inside, Doc." With measured steps he made his way to the door leading into the house.

Gordie didn't raise her head, didn't want to see they were in the garage with the door wide open where anyone could see them. She'd always known it would be like this. Knew the minute Steve touched her she'd forget everything and everyone —forget herself.

STEVE MADE it inside and to his room in record time. He was on a hair trigger and Doc wasn't helping with the way she'd wrapped herself around him and kept nibbling on his neck with those sweet lips. Jesus, he couldn't remember why he'd thought this wasn't a good idea yet. There had been a very good reason to wait until after everyone had gone home but for the life of him he couldn't think of it.

They entered his room, a memory of the last time he'd carried her through the doorway intruded and he ruthlessly shoved it back. Steve strode across the room, his gaze locked on the bathroom. He kicked the door shut behind them, the bang echoed off the walls and brought Doc's head up, her gaze connecting with his.

"Shower." Steve ground the word out through clenched

teeth as he set her on her feet. "I'll bring you some clothes to wear."

"You're leaving?"

He closed his eyes, his control held by a thread. "If I don't I'm taking you against the wall and I want more time to explore you than a quick fuck in the shower."

"But you made me come."

"Yeah, and I will again, just not yet." Steve opened his eyes to see Doc removing her top. The sexy, white lace bra beneath her blue blouse was made of pure sin. A groan gurgled in his throat. "Christ."

Her hands stilled on the button of her pants and she raised her gaze to his. She studied him with her doctor stare. He knew what she was doing—analyzing, thinking, planning. Damn, that mind of hers was as sexy as her underwear.

He took a step back, reached behind him for the door handle and Doc got right up in his face, her hand pressed to the door behind him as though she could stop him from opening it.

"Get your clothes off now," she demanded.

Steve smiled. "Back to being disagreeable, Doc?"

"You are not leaving this bathroom before I mark you. I don't care if we have sex, I give you a blowjob or a hand job. One way or another you will leave this bathroom mine as I entered it yours."

His cock went rock hard. Her take-charge attitude thrilled him and he couldn't wait to be on the receiving end of any one of those suggestions. "Bossy much, Doc?"

"You like it."

He arched an eyebrow. "Really?"

Doc wrapped her hand around his length through his jeans. "Oh yeah, you like it."

They stared at each other, gauging who would give first. Only the fight was one-sided. Her fingers squeezed and stroked him and even with the denim barrier her touch set his blood on fire. His coyote howled for him to take what she offered while he fought to keep his civility and not rut on her like the beast he was. Control snapped and he glanced at his watch.

"I reckon we have five minutes before anyone shows up and it shames me to say I won't need that long." He gripped her shoulders, pushed her back. "Strip."

She stumbled, caught herself and kicked off her shoes. Her pants came next but he missed the unveiling of her panties as he pulled his shirt over his head. Steve's breath snagged in his chest when he spotted the matching underwear. Dear God, she'd kill him without laying a hand on him. He went to work on his pants, his cock sprang free and Doc dropped to her knees in front of him, her hot breath bathed the head seconds before she swallowed him whole.

"Fuck!"

Doc took him in as deep as she could. The crown bumped against the back of her throat and dragged a groan from his gut. One hand worked his balls, rolling them, tugging, rubbing the sensitive skin beneath. The other gripped the base of his shaft, pumping up and down, matching the rhythm of her mouth. Shit, he wouldn't last a minute, never mind five. She undid him, her lips, her tongue, the grasp of her throat, all designed to drive him out of his mind. He clenched his jaw—his ass cheeks—in his fight not to come.

Damn, he didn't want to do it like this. He wanted inside her cunt, wanted to bathe her womb with his seed and mark her completely as his. With strength he didn't think he had, Steve pulled from Doc's mouth.

"No, not this way the first time." He tugged her to her feet. "Turn around, hold the counter and spread your legs."

She did as asked, even tilted her hips to shove her ass in his direction. Steve toed off his boots and kicked his jeans aside.

Stepping between her feet, he bent his knees and lined his cock up with her pussy. The slick evidence of her recent orgasm coated her folds, made the slide inside easy. He rocked forward, pushed deeper and concentrated on not embarrassing himself. Heat engulfed him, her tight walls sucking at his length like her mouth had moments before.

Steve adjusted his feet, brought their bodies more in line and drove his shaft to the hilt. Doc stood on her toes, thrust her hips back and met him stroke for stroke as he began to fuck her in earnest. Deep, hard, long plunges in. Short, sharp retreats. He built the rhythm, pulled her with him as he sought the peak. Curling over her back, he pressed his chest to her spine and slid a hand over her stomach to the juncture of her thighs.

He found her clit, hard and protruding from its protective hood, and circled the wet bundle with a fingertip. Increasing the pressure in small increments, he pushed her toward release. Her inner walls convulsed, a ripple of hot velvet along his probing length like a thousand tongues. His sac tightened, pulled his balls up and Steve knew he was on the verge of coming. Wanting her with him when he went over the edge he doubled his efforts on the nub beneath his finger and sank his teeth into the side of her neck.

Doc bucked against him. Her orgasm slammed into both of them. She squeezed his cock, held it prisoner in her clenching body. Steve's balls burst into flame, shooting hot cum through his shaft and filling her core. Each blast burned his flesh, caused her walls to clamp harder around him, sucking the breath from his lungs. His knees shook, threatened to collapse, and he braced his arm, his palm flat on the counter in front of them.

Their chests heaved with their labored breaths, the harsh sound of rushing air bouncing off the walls around them. He found the strength to lift up, pull his softening cock from her body and step back. Reaching out, he turned the water on so they could clean up. They were running out of time if they wanted to be dressed when the others arrived.

"Come on, Doc, let's get showered and dressed before company arrives."

He wrapped his arm around her waist and picked her up off her feet. She was such a tiny thing compared to him but her size belied her strength. He'd seen her deal with guys almost as big as him. At the moment though, she was as weak as a kitten and allowed him to pull her under the running water without protest.

"It won't matter."

He had to lean over to hear her words above the pounding spray. "What won't?"

"Whether we're dressed or not." She raised her gaze to meet his. "They'll all know."

"Is that a problem?"

She smiled. "No."

Steve bent down, pressed his lips to hers. A chaste kiss by any standard, he moved his mouth against hers, brushing back and forth in light caresses. Their mouths melded, their tongues barely coming into play. Soft and easy, they came together, their bodies, slick from the shower, sliding, skin on skin. Hands roamed in gentle sweeps, sending fire through his veins all over again. Breaking away, he gasped for air and laid his forehead on hers.

"Damn. I'm not gonna get enough of you anytime soon. Good thing it's Christmas and you've got the next week off because once everyone clears out tonight I'm getting you naked and in that bed out there and not letting you up until I've had my fill."

"I'm a little shocked to admit I feel the same." She stepped back, breaking their embrace completely. "Let's get this over with so we can get on with our week."

Doc turned her back and bent under the spray to wet her hair. He reached over her head for the shampoo and handed it to her. Grabbing the soap he made short work of cleaning up before helping her. Steve ran his bubble-lathered hands across every inch of her. By the time they were finished he was sporting a hard-on and wished he didn't have to deal with the people arriving any minute even if they were his friends and he'd called them in.

Steve sighed as he stepped out of the shower and snagged a towel off the rail. He slung it around his hips and picked up a second one for Doc. She shut off the water and walked into his arms.

"It won't be long, you know." She stood on her tiptoes and kissed the end of his nose.

The action was so surprising that Steve stood paralyzed for long seconds.

"What's wrong?" She arched an eyebrow. "Ah. No one's ever kissed you on the nose before."

How did she read him so well? They'd been friends since she'd arrived in the mountains with her mother all those years ago but still, she seemed to understand him on a level no one ever had. Always knew when he'd reached his limit and backed away.

He shrugged. "No actually, they haven't."

"Good." Her lips curled in a smug smile.

"Why is that good?"

"Because it means we get to have a first together."

"Doc, we're going to have lots of firsts before we're done." He slapped her towel-covered butt. "Now get a move on. We've got guests coming."

Steve ushered her out of the bathroom and over to his dresser. Pulling out a drawer, he found her a t-shirt and sweatpants with a drawstring waist so she could cinch it tight to hold them up. She put the shirt on first and the hem came to her knees. If it wasn't for their expected company he'd snatch the pants back and make her wear only his shirt.

"Stop grinning. I'm not leaving the pants off."

There she went again with that mind-reading thing.

"How do you know that's what I'm thinking?"

"It's in your eyes." She glanced up at him as she bent to pull on the sweats. "You get this look of hunger that my mind has no trouble understanding."

"Nice to know I'm so easily read."

"You're not the only one. Everyone's emotions show in their eyes." She shrugged. "I guess I've just learned to look closely over time."

"I don't seem to be able to read you as well."

"Another thing I've learned over the years."

"What?"

"It's called a poker face. I learned early to hide my emotions."

"I know what a poker face is but why would you need one?"

Her fingers twisted in the bow she'd tied the drawstring in. Doc may have perfected a poker face but her actions and body posture gave her away.

"Doc?"

"As a doctor I need to keep my emotions locked away or I'd never survive my job."

"You were unreadable long before you became a doctor." He studied her, tried to see past the shields in her eyes but as usual, failed. "You don't just wear your poker face at work do you, Doc? You have it on all the time. Why is that?"

She laughed, but the brittle sound held no trace of humor. "You think I could grow up in this town without hiding how I felt? It's not easy being the odd man out when you're a kid."

"Gordie, you've never been odd man—"

She held up her hand. "Yes I have. No other person has lived as a human in this town for as long as I did. *Ever.* That alone makes me odd. The fact I married Anthony when I shouldn't have, plus what happened after, just adds to my list of peculiar attributes. I've spent years trying to put all that behind me, there's no way I'll drop my guard and risk starting up another round of whispering for the town to enjoy."

He pulled her into his arms. "You're not odd and no one has ever really looked at you that way. And believe me, you don't need to do anything to become fodder for the rumor mill in Whispering Springs. I've spent years listening to the old-timers chatter at your sister's café and there's plenty that goes on in these mountains for them to talk about besides you. Come to think of it, I don't think they've mentioned you in years."

Doc laughed and shoved away from him. "You idiot. No one is game to talk about me in front of you."

"What? Why?" He crossed his arms over his chest.

"Because you give the evil eye better than the devil himself."

He snarled. "I do not."

This time when she laughed she doubled over and held her ribs. Gasping for breath, she said, "Go look in the mirror, you idiot."

Steve knew what he'd see. There was no controlling the way he reacted whenever he thought of Doc and he hadn't bothered to hide that from anyone since her return to town. And now he'd have the right to show that reaction. He smiled. Oh yeah, the town would soon know whom she belonged to.

"And don't go getting that look."

"What look?"

"That *she's mine, keep away* look."

Damn, she really could read him as easy as a book. "It's the truth and I'm not hiding it ever again." He cupped her cheek in his palm, pleased when she turned into the caress. "I want everyone to know you're mine."

"They already know." She sighed. "They've just been waiting for me to give in."

"And did you give in, Doc?"

"No, I took." She grinned.

"Yes, you sure did. And you did such a good job. I feel all used."

A giggle slipped past her lips, the sound so girlish Steve was reminded of years past when they hung out with the same group in high school.

"I like the sound of that. I want to hear you laugh like that more often," he said.

"Hang around, McKenna and you just might get that wish."

"Oh, I'll be hanging. I'm not planning on going anywhere that isn't with you."

"You're such a sweet talker."

"I can talk lots of ways. After everyone leaves I'll show you my dirty talk." He waggled his eyebrows and licked his lips making a slurping noise.

"Eww... I hope you mean sexy dirty talk or I'm outta here."

Steve wrapped his arm around her neck and dragged her back to his side. "Definitely sexy dirty talk, Doc. Now let's go wait for our company."

He felt her stiffen against him and knew she was thinking about what she'd have to reveal. As much as he wanted to take away her worry he knew she had to do this. He'd stand beside her and support her as best he could but he couldn't fight all her battles no matter how badly he wanted to.

3

THEY'D REACHED the main area of the house when someone knocked on Steve's front door and continued to knock.

"Let me guess." Steve let her go and walked over to unlock the deadbolt. "This'll be Kat."

As soon as the door opened her sister charged past Steve as if he didn't exist. Kat spanned the gap between them in less than a second and threw her arms around Gordie's neck.

"Thank God, you're okay."

"I'm fine, Kat." Gordie smiled at Steve over her sister's head. "Unless you plan to choke me to death."

Kat eased up on her grip but didn't let go. "Give me a sec. I just need to know you're all right."

Gordie could allow her sister that much. While they hugged in Steve's foyer, Rowan came through the door carrying bags of food. One by one the others came in out of the cold, all of them laden down with groceries. Dale was the last to arrive, murmuring something to Steve as he closed the door behind everyone.

"Come on, Kat. Let your sister go so we can eat all this food you made us drag up here," Rowan said.

"I bought..." Kat sniffled. She leaned back and looked at Gordie with one arched eyebrow. "Well, I'll be." Her sister took a deep breath and smiled. "About damn time, too."

She knew what Kat could smell but this wasn't the time or the place for that conversation. "Not now."

"We've all waited years for you two to get it on. You should be yelling it from the rooftop."

"Shh. I don't want to talk about it at the moment."

"Oh come on, Gordie. You guys have been dancing around each other since you came home years ago. Everyone is going to be thrilled that you finally gave in."

"Kat! I did not—"

"Sure you did, the whole town knows you're the one fighting it."

"Enough, Kat." Steve's quiet words didn't hide the hard edge they were delivered with.

Gordie watched Kat wrestle her need to argue. The girl could argue under wet concrete and she still didn't know why her sister had given up her dream of being a lawyer and taken over The Dec Café from their Granny Roe. She'd probably never find out. Even though Kat was the first to ferret out other people's secrets, she kept her own locked in a vault, not even Gordie was privy to what lay hidden behind that sealed door.

"I brought stew for tonight. I also packed up a heap of groceries, lasagna and a chicken pie. But don't think all this food gives you reason to stay up here Christmas Day. I want to see you both at my place for lunch with presents in hand." Kat marched toward the kitchen.

"She's like this every day isn't she?" Steve asked, shaking his head.

With a sigh, Gordie turned to face him. "Yeah, she is."

"I've seen her take charge of things at the café but have never been subjected to it personally. Did she really bring all that food?"

Gordie laughed. "You saw the bags everyone carted in. Kat's always had this need to feed anything with a mouth. We used to joke when she was little about her finding a mate early and having a truckload of kids to mother." Gordie stared after her sister. "You know I don't think I've seen her date anyone since she was in high school."

"And that's a subject we're not touching." He placed a hand on her lower back and gently nudged her forward. "Come on, we've put it off long enough."

The next few minutes were taken up by Kat giving orders and everyone following them. Bowls were filled with hot stew, and with food in hand they went into the dining room where Steve's hand-carved table and chairs seated all of them with room to spare. Gordie ate a mouthful of food and chewed. Usually her sister's cooking tasted delicious but she could have been eating dirt for all the flavor she could taste tonight.

There was no point putting it off any longer, it wouldn't get any easier. She just had to decide where to start, what was necessary and what she was comfortable disclosing. Pushing her bowl away, Gordie leaned back in her chair and turned her head to catch Steve's gaze. He slipped his hand over hers and gave a gentle squeeze before returning to his meal.

"It started last year when I found the first stray up here. That's the first significant event I can remember, anyway. After that there was all the drama of Rowan's return and the attempt on Quinn's life by the other two strays and of course Malcolm trying to run him down." She reached for her water and took a sip to wet her dry mouth and throat.

"Between January and May there were numerous little things, objects moved in my house and at the clinic, doors unlocked when I was sure I'd locked them, missing papers from my home office, that sort of thing." Gordie took a deep breath and glanced at Steve. He reached for her hand again, entwined their fingers and nodded for her to go on. She kept her gaze locked with his. If she looked away she knew the words wouldn't come.

"May eighteenth I came up here to walk in the forest. I was going to shift, go for a run but decided against it." She swallowed over the lump in her throat. "I didn't hear anything or see anyone before I took a punch to the jaw. The force snapped my head back into a tree. I don't remember a lot of the next few minutes other than I took some hits before I caught my breath and fought back. I never saw who attacked me and whoever it was had masked their scent well enough that I couldn't say for sure who it was."

Gordie trembled. Memories of that night bombarded her, fear churned the food in her stomach and she had to swallow the bile rising in her throat. A chair scraped along the timber floor and Steve pulled her onto his lap, cradling her against his chest. He kissed the top of her head and held her close, warmth seeped from his body into hers, soothing her. She couldn't stop shaking and her fingers and toes were numb from the cold gripping her.

"The details don't matter, Gordie." Steve tucked her head under his chin. "I'll finish this part, okay?"

Gordie nodded. She didn't dare open her mouth to speak for fear a sob would tear free. Or worse, she'd throw up. In the months since the attack she'd done her best to block the whole event out. But in her effort to forget the horrible night she'd pushed the person who saved her and cared for her afterward away as well. It was unfair to Steve but at the time she couldn't cope any other way.

"I heard the attack from the deck so I shifted and ran into

the forest. I didn't see who had Doc pinned to the ground but at the time she thought it was Marcus."

Steve's words were met with gasps but it was Brogan's softly spoken words that froze Gordie. The venom in them turned her blood to ice.

"I should have killed him when I had the chance."

"No, Gordie and Steve should have reported the attack," Dale said.

"Probably." She felt Steve's shoulders rise. "But to be honest, I was more concerned with looking after Doc's injuries, and we had no real proof."

"Oh my God, the scar on your lip." Gordie opened her eyes to find Kat kneeling on the floor beside her. "You told me you'd sliced it with a knife while eating fruit."

She tried to smile but the hurt in her sister's eyes stopped her. "I'm sorry. I just wanted to forget. And nothing happened after that."

"Until last month." Warm air ruffled her hair. "What happened, Doc? And don't tell me nothing because I know you, I know something's been going on for weeks now."

Gordie sighed and sat up to face the others. "The week before El arrived in Whispering Springs my house was broken into but unlike before it was obvious. Whoever it was smashed out the kitchen window." She turned to Dale. "And before you ask, nothing was taken. I don't know what the aim was, to frighten me maybe. They took nothing but went out of their way to let me know they'd been inside by messing with my things."

A growl rumbled behind her. She expected to face an angry Steve at some point, hopefully he'd hold it all in until everyone went home. She knew keeping everything from him was wrong but she couldn't change that now.

"Go on. What else?" Dale asked.

"Nothing until after the wedding." Gordie glanced at Rowan. "It started with little things being moved, food missing, doors unlocked when they shouldn't have been. Clothes that aren't mine laid out on my bed."

"What the fuck?" Steve spun her around on his lap until they were nose to nose. "Some fucking prick was in your bedroom and you never told me!"

"That only happened yesterday. I haven't seen you to tell you." As much as she'd wanted to call him last night, her sister had been with her when she'd arrived home and made the discovery. If she hadn't convinced Kat to stay she would have phoned him. "Kat was with me."

"You found that last night and didn't say anything? Jesus, Gordana, what were you thinking?" Kat gripped Gordie's leg and gave it a shake.

"I didn't want you to worry. If you hadn't stayed I would have called Steve."

"You should have called me regardless."

"Whose clothes were they?"

Gordie turned to Rowan. She could tell by her friend's white face and wide eyes that Rowan knew the answer. "Yours."

"Bullshit! What clothes?" Quinn stood, his chair toppled over, hit the floor with a loud crash. He stared down at Rowan.

Rowan never broke eye contact with Gordie. "My mother's wedding dress."

"Fuck off!" Brogan rose to his feet. "How the hell did that end up in Gordie's house?"

"It wasn't at the cleaners when I went to pick it up last week. They thought it was still out being cleaned but Nancy had phoned to tell me it was ready so I knew something wasn't right. I was hoping they'd just misplaced it."

Brogan turned to El. "And your dress? You put it in with Rowan's."

El licked her lips. Glanced at Gordie and Rowan in turn. "I... I don't know. It's missing too."

"Except Rowan's isn't missing anymore," Dale said.

"No, it's in my closet."

"What I don't get is why leave Rowan's dress at Gordie's? There doesn't seem to be a purpose to it." Kat's head tilted at an angle and she got that look of concentration she wore whenever she thought hard about something. "Do you think this is about getting everyone involved? I mean, before yesterday it all seemed focused on Gordie but add in this dress thing and he's pulling someone else into the equation."

"This isn't math, Kat. Besides, it's Marcus we're talking about, who knows what goes through that twisted head of his," Steve said.

"No, Kat's right. All Marcus' previous actions have targeted individuals, there was no crossover except when Rowan returned and I think that was accidental more than on purpose. This is different. I'm not sure how or why but the game rules have changed," Dale added.

"So what do we do now?" Gordie looked at Dale.

"I want to have a look at your house and I'd like to go back to the clinic in daylight. Do you mind if I do that while you're closed?"

"No, go ahead." Gordie got to her feet. "I'll get you my keys. Quinn do you have the new keys for the clinic?"

"Dale has them."

"Okay." She stifled a yawn. "Sorry, I think it's catching up with me. I'll just go grab those keys."

"Gordie, go on to bed. I'll make sure Dale gets the keys," Steve said.

"I'm fine, just a little tired and my feet are cold."

Steve stood and scooped her up in his arms.

"Hey."

"Hey, yourself."

"Put me down."

"I will." He walked across the room. "Just as soon as I get you in the bedroom. Say goodnight, Gordie."

A chorus of *goodnight Gordie* echoed behind them as Steve strode along the hallway leading to the bedroom.

Gordie yawned again. She really was tired. Maybe she'd just lie down for a few minutes. Steve deposited her on the mattress and stood with hands on hips beside the bed.

"No arguing, you've got dark circles under your eyes. I bet you didn't sleep at all last night, did you?"

She ducked her head. There was no way she could sleep after finding that dress on her bed, not even with her sister in the room down the hall. "No."

"Just as I thought." He reached over and pulled the covers back. "Come on, ditch the pants and climb in."

"Ditch the pants?"

"You can't sleep in those. Leave the shirt on though, it gets chilly even with the heat on."

Before she could move he'd snagged the end of the bow and yanked the drawstring loose. Gripping a bunch of fabric in each fist at her hips he tugged the sweats down her legs and threw them in the general direction of the dresser.

"There. Climb in. I'll go see to our friends and be back before you've missed me."

"Who said I'd miss you?" She smiled around another yawn and her eyelids grew heavy.

"Me." Steve bent over and gave her a smacking kiss on the mouth. "Rest. I'll be right down the hall."

"Rest with me." Her eyes closed.

"Later."

"Okay."

"Back to agreeable Doc, I see."

"Only until I sleep."

Steve chuckled. "Doesn't matter which Doc you are, I'm still glad you're in my bed."

"You just liked the sex."

"Gordie." His fingers brushed her cheek.

"Mmm..."

"Sleep."

"Night."

STEVE GAZED down at a sleeping Doc and tried not to climb into bed with her. He still had to go out and deal with their friends and he wanted to be sure Dale kept him in the loop about her house and the clinic. Anger still burned in his gut when he thought about her not calling him last night. She wouldn't admit it but she was still holding him at arm's length. A smile stretched his mouth. There would be no holding him off now.

Doc was right, he had enjoyed the sex but it had been far more than a physical act. He'd finally been buried inside her after years of dreaming about it. No fantasy he'd concocted came close to the real thing. Now he wanted a repeat but she needed to rest and he had to sort out a plan of defense because there was no doubt in his mind that Marcus was back on the scene. In fact, Steve was pretty sure the man had never left.

He tiptoed from the room and pulled the door shut, leaving it open a crack so he could hear Doc if she called out. Quiet voices drifted down the hall, they grew louder as he made his way back to the dining room. The table had been cleared and everyone sat with a mug of coffee, at least he thought that's what he smelled. Obviously Kat's talents weren't just with food.

"How is she?" Kat asked.

"Asleep." She eyed him through narrowed lids. He knew what she was really asking but he wasn't getting into that with her. "Later."

Steve spied a spare mug and picked it up. The aroma rose up, teasing his senses with the taste to come. He sipped, the hot liquid filling his mouth, spilling over his tongue. Damn, whoever made this knew what they were doing. Taking a bigger drink he walked out of the room and headed for the garage. They'd left Doc's purse in his truck when they rushed inside earlier. He placed his mug on the table beside the garage door as he walked past.

He retrieved her bag from the truck and headed for the button to shut the roller door and pressed it, but movement at the end of the driveway caught his eye and he quickly aborted the action. Peering into the night, Steve tried to focus but the lack of light outside and the abundance of it inside combined to make it impossible. He stepped to the edge of the garage for a better look when he heard someone behind him. Spinning on his heels, fists raised, he came face-to-face with Dale.

"Sorry, didn't mean to startle you."

"No worries, I'm a little jumpy."

"That's expected. What are you doing?"

Steve pointed down the driveway. "What is that?"

Dale leaned forward. "You got floodlights?"

"Yeah, let me get the switch." Steve strode to the other side of his truck and flicked a couple of levers. Light illuminated the entire front yard.

"Shit!" Dale took off running.

"What the fuck?" Steve dropped Doc's purse and raced after the sheriff.

The new layer of snow on the ground proved difficult to traverse and they slipped and slid their way to the end of the drive. They skidded to a halt as a woman wobbled and lost her footing in the slippery conditions, crumpling beside Dale's car. At least Steve thought it was a female bundled up under all that snow gear.

He crouched down and gripped her shoulder. "Hey, are you all right?"

"C-c-cold." Her voice was muffled by the beanie pulled down low on her forehead and the scarf wrapped around to cover what was left of her face, but neither could hide the chattering of her teeth.

Steve pushed the cold, wet material aside. "Recognize her?" he asked Dale.

His friend sucked in a breath as he squatted beside him. "Tatum. It's Tatum Brant. William's granddaughter. But she hasn't been back in the mountain for years."

"Let's get her inside out of the weather." Steve slid his arm around her as best he could with the bulky jacket she wore. He lifted and Dale steadied them as they got to their feet.

One on either side of her, they headed back to the house. She trembled against him and Steve could feel the damp and cold seeping from her clothes to his. It was awkward, she seemed to be wearing a wardrobe full of clothes beneath her thick coat. They reached the garage and crossed to the connecting door where Brogan and Quinn met them.

"Who the hell is that?" Quinn asked.

"Tatum Brant," Dale answered.

"Where'd she come from?" Brogan asked.

"Bottom of the driveway, she was trying to make it to the house," Steve said. "Can you go shut the garage door and turn off all the lights, Quinn?"

"Sure."

"Oh, and Doc's bag is on the ground near the light switches."

"Got it."

Her trembling had turned into bone-rattling shakes by the time Steve guided them into the living room where he and Dale lowered Tatum to the couch. He began removing her wet outerwear and quickly discovered the reason for her bulky mass. The women came in from the kitchen and immediately rushed over.

"Jesus. Is that...?" Kat asked.

"Tatum Brant," Steve said.

"Is she...?" Doc's sister seemed to be having problems forming complete sentences.

"Pregnant?" Steve finished for her.

"I haven't seen her in years. How'd she get here?"

"No idea and right now my priority is getting her warm," Steve said.

Tatum tried to curl up but her protruding belly hampered her efforts. Dale sat next to her and pulled her against his side. He wrapped his arms around her as best he could and ran his hands up and down her back. "You got a blanket, Steve?"

"Yeah, let me grab one. I'll turn the heat up too."

Steve left the room. After pulling a couple of quilts from the linen cupboard and returning them to the living room, he detoured to his room to check on Doc. She was exactly where he'd left her, sound asleep with one hand tucked under her cheek. The dark circles under her eyes made her face look bruised and he vowed to spend the next week making sure she got plenty of rest so those black smudges disappeared completely. He pulled the covers up over her shoulders and bent down to drop a light kiss on her forehead. Breathing deep, he drew her scent into his lungs.

Memories of earlier flashed through his mind. His cock

hardened and a groan rumbled in his chest. There wouldn't be a repeat performance any time soon. Not with everyone still here and Doc in need of sleep. With a sigh, he straightened and forced himself to turn and leave the room. Each step dragged and he wondered at the irony of the moment. He'd waited so long for her to acknowledge their attraction and when she did everything and everyone seemed to be getting in the way of them being together.

As he approached the living room, he could hear raised voices. They got louder the closer he got and he quickened his pace, determined to stop them before it became a yelling match.

"Hey, keep it down, you'll wake Doc."

The sight before him amused and confused him. Dale stood with the pint-sized Tatum right up in his face. For someone who'd barely functioned a few minutes ago, she'd made a swift recovery. She'd backed the sheriff up against the wall and had a finger prodding him in the chest. Both turned toward him as he entered the room.

"What's going on?" he asked.

"Doc *is* here?" Tatum stepped away from Dale.

Dale grabbed her by the arm. "I told you you weren't seeing her tonight."

"And I told you to stop manhandling me." She tried to pry his fingers from her skin. "I'd hate to see how you treat criminals if this is how law-abiding citizens are handled."

The sheriff dropped her arm like it was a hot rock. "Tatum."

"Sheriff."

Steve watched as they stared each other down and much to his surprise Dale broke away first. He watched the sheriff close his eyes and run a hand down his face. "Tatum, Doc is resting. She had a...scare earlier and isn't up to seeing a patient."

"I'm not a patient. But you haven't given me two seconds to explain myself so it's no wonder you've jumped to the wrong conclusion."

"Tatum, what were you doing out on the road?" Steve asked.

"I came up here after I called in at the café. The woman behind the counter said Doc and Kat were here and she thought Doc might need me," she explained.

"Need you?"

"I'm a nurse. Doc's nurse, actually, but I'm not due to start until after the fifteenth of next month." She walked over to the couch, one hand pressed to the small of her back making her pregnant belly stick out more. Slowly, she lowered to the cushions. "Damn, I must have pulled something trudging through the snow."

"You walked up here?" Dale barked.

"No, stupid. I drove, but I slid on some ice about ten minutes down the road and ended up in a ditch. I walked the rest of the way but then it started to snow and I got colder by the second. I'd just popped the lock on the cop car out front when you two came to my rescue."

"You broke into my car?"

Steve smiled. Tatum didn't seem like such a law-abiding citizen right now. She ignored Dale and kept on with her story.

"Look, I know this is strange but the woman at the café made it sound as if Doc had been hurt and I couldn't just go on over to Gramps' house without checking she was all right." She slumped back against the couch with a sigh. "By the time I reached the end of the driveway my legs were shaking with exhaustion as well as the cold and I was worried I'd collapse in the snow. I thought if I could flip on the siren someone would hear."

"I'm sorry Wendy worried you and put you in danger, but Doc isn't hurt," Steve said.

"Um…Steve?"

"What?" He turned to look behind him at Kat.

"How many bedrooms does this place have?" Kat asked.

"Four. Why?" He glanced past Kat and through the windows running the length of the room. "Oh shit."

"Yeah, that's what I was thinking," Kat said.

He walked over to join her. On the other side of the glass he could see the deck, along with the rapidly accumulating layer of snow covering it. More snow fell in a thick blanket that blocked out the view of the timber railing twenty feet away, never mind the forest beyond.

"Damn. Doesn't look good." Brogan stepped up next to him. "Does anyone know what the weather's supposed to be like?"

"Yeah, we're due for a storm tomorrow. Looks like it moved in early," Dale answered.

"Jesus. I guess I'll go drag out the extra bedding." Steve turned from the window. "How many of us are there?"

"I can share with Kat if she's all right with that and it makes things easier," Tatum said.

"I'm fine with that but don't you dare have that baby in the bed next to me." Kat glared at her.

Tatum laughed. "It's babies and they're not due for another three months."

Dale made a choking sound next to him and Steve turned to see a red-faced sheriff.

"Three months? You look like you're ready to pop now." Rowan sat on the couch next to Tatum. "So you're about four months ahead of me then. And El's pregnant too, but only just. Looks like there'll be lots of new babies next year."

"Tatum, can I have a word please?" Dale walked over and reached for her hand. "In private."

Steve thought he saw her hesitate but then she placed her hand in Dale's and allowed him to pull her to her feet, quickly disengaging their hands when she was steady. His friend seemed lost for a moment and Steve realized he had no idea where to go to have their talk.

"Down the hall, first door on the left is my office. You can use that if you like," Steve offered.

"Thanks. I'll bunk on the couch tonight. Just toss some blankets out and I'll fix it up when I'm ready," Dale said.

"No need. The sofa in the office is a pull-out. Everyone else can take a bedroom."

"Oh, okay. We'll be back in a minute." Dale gripped Tatum's elbow and all but dragged her out of the room.

Steve couldn't help think there was more going on with that pair but he couldn't see how when Tatum hadn't been in the mountains for years and was obviously pregnant with someone's babies.

"Hey, what's up with those two?" Kat asked next to him.

"Don't know and right now I've got more pressing things to think about." He turned to Brogan. "You and El can take the first room on the right down the hall. Quinn and Rowan take the next one and Kat, you and Tatum can share the one across from that. There's extra bedding in the wardrobes. I think I might have spare toothbrushes somewhere too."

Rowan stood and stretched. "I'm beat. Anyone mind if I call it a night?"

"I'm thinking the same thing. Kat, do you need any more help in the kitchen?" El asked.

"No. I just have to load and start the dishwasher. Go on to bed. You've both got baby growing to do."

Steve tuned out the women's conversation and walked back over to the window. He stared out beyond the glass at the wall of white. The snowfall had grown heavier in the last few minutes. If it kept up for long no one would be leaving tomorrow. As long as the storm blew over before morning he could get the plow out and lead them all down the mountain road back to town, but if it continued past sunrise he'd be stuck with his unwanted guests another night.

WARM ARMS SLIPPED around her waist and Gordie snuggled back against the hard chest pressing in behind her. Soft lips traveled over her exposed neck, sending shivers down her spine.

"Mmm... What time is it?"

"Early. Everyone's gone to bed."

"Everyone?"

Steve sighed, his hot breath bathing her ear. "Yeah, tomorrow's expected snowstorm blew in early. We're stuck with them until morning."

"Oh."

"Don't worry. The minute the snow stops I'll get the plow out and clear the road into town. I guess all that food your sister brought with her will come in handy now."

"Good thing she did bring it, you don't have much in your fridge."

"There's plenty in the chest freezer downstairs." Steve grazed his teeth along her shoulder. "But enough about food. I have a different appetite I want to satisfy."

He trailed his tongue along the shell of her ear before sucking the lobe between his lips and nipping with his teeth. She arched into him and her bottom cradled his erection, the hard length pressing into the crease between her cheeks. Heat pooled in her abdomen and moisture coated her folds. Gordie wriggled around until she faced him. Reaching up, she ran her fingers through his hair.

"Hi."

"Hi, yourself."

She smiled. "Did I miss anything important?"

"Yeah. This." Steve lowered his head and kissed her.

At first he kept the kiss slow and easy but it soon wasn't enough for either of them and he thrust his tongue between her lips to probe inside. She met him stroke for stroke, demand for demand. Sucking hard, Gordie pulled his tongue deeper, used her teeth to scrape the sides as she let go. Steve groaned into her mouth and angled his head for a better fit.

Gordie splayed her fingers on his chest, the hot muscles rippled as she explored his body. Moving her hands lower, she toyed with the washboard abs he'd earned from honest work. She detoured farther south, to his narrow hips and the delicious valleys leading the way to the prize hidden between his legs.

Steve's mouth left hers to graze over her chin and down her throat. He nipped at her collarbone, licked to soothe the slight sting before moving to the other side and repeating his actions, making her gasp. Her fingers curled around his hips, her nails digging in, and his pelvis bucked toward her. His cock rubbed over her clit, the material of her shirt abrading the sensitive nub setting off sparks of delight.

She moaned and moved with him, rocked to find the friction she needed. Her pussy clenched and spasmed with longing and Gordie increased the pace. Steve tugged at her shirt with his teeth, pulled it off her shoulder to lick the skin beneath. Frustrated by the barrier between them, she shoved him away and turned to wiggle out of the top. He helped and in their haste the cloth tore apart at the seam.

He wrenched her free and tossed the shirt over his shoulder. In a second he rolled her under him, slipped his knee between hers and spread her legs wide. His thighs brushed hers, the rough hair tickling her soft skin. Gordie lifted her pelvis to bring her sex in direct contact with his shaft. Hot and hard, the silky length slid along her slick folds, bumping her pulsing clit. She cried out and he covered her mouth with his hand.

"Shh. They'll hear you."

Gordie sucked her lips between her teeth, bit down to hold them in place and nodded. Steve removed his hand and gripped her chin.

"I want to hear you scream. Want to hear my name on your lips when I make you come, but I don't want anyone else hearing that cry of pleasure. That's mine and mine alone."

Steve didn't give her a chance to answer. His mouth covered hers in a punishing kiss meant to claim. He flexed his hips and brought his cock to her opening. Pressing forward, he entered her, breaching her body slowly. She wanted more—all of him. Gordie thrust up and drove his shaft deeper, wrenching a moan from each of them. They moved together, built a rhythm of give and take that quickly grew in speed and strength.

She gnawed on her lips, held them tight between her teeth to muffle the cries of pleasure she couldn't control. Steve's hands circled her hips, his fingers spread over her ass cheeks. He held her still, pinned to the bed, and drove in hard, his length dragging over her swollen clit with every stroke. Her head tossed on the pillow and her nails dug into his shoulders as her orgasm built inside her, tightening with each plunge, every retreat of his cock.

"Please." Gordie hooked her legs over his hips. "Steve."

Her words spurred him on. He pounded into her, pushed

them both to the edge as their bodies slammed together—strived for release.

"Touch yourself." His hoarse demand sent a bolt of fire into her core. "Do it."

Gordie slipped her hand between them, her fingers searching for the spot that would bring her relief. She encountered wet heat and probed farther. Cream coated her fingertips as she circled them over her clit, applied a little pressure and brought herself closer to the peak.

Steve leaned on his elbows and lifted up to look at where their bodies were joined. "God, that's so hot. Watching you get yourself off is a huge turn-on, Doc."

He pulled back and Gordie reached lower to graze her fingernails along his length as he withdrew.

"Fuck!" He slammed forward, trapping her hand between them. "Do that again," he growled.

She twisted her hand slightly, used her fingers on his cock and her thumb on her clit, and drove them both insane. Steve jerked, his rhythm erratic for a couple of strokes before he returned to the beat, this time faster. Harder. The first contraction rolled into the second and onto the third, her whole body flowing with the waves of her orgasm as they took her under and dragged him with her.

"Steve."

He continued to drive into her, pushing deeper with each splash of warmth filling her core. Burying his face in the curve of her neck he called her name, the sound more groan than word. Gasping for breath, Gordie held onto him, his weight pressing her into the bedding. Her limbs tingled, whether from lack of circulation or oxygen it didn't matter and she didn't care.

"Too heavy," he murmured against her skin, sending ripples of goose bumps skittering down her neck.

"No. I like feeling your weight crush me."

"Gee, Doc, you say the sweetest things." He grinned against her throat.

"You know what I mean," she sighed.

"Yes I do but you're so fun to tease."

"Really? Well just as long as you can take it as well as dish it."

"Bring it, Doc. I'll take all you've got."

He bucked his hips, his cock, still buried inside her, scraped over tender tissues. Her pussy throbbed, clamped around him.

"Ooh." Steve lifted his head and met her gaze. "Again?"

She arched a brow. "Now?"

His hips rocked, his hardening length pumping in and out. "Yeah. Now."

"Okay, but I'm on top this time." Gordie tried to roll them but he held her beneath him easily.

"You gonna ride me, Doc?"

"Not from dow—"

Her head spun and hair flopped in front of her face. She shoved the strands aside with one hand, gripped his biceps to steady herself with the other and stared down at him. "How the hell did you do that?"

"Be a good girl and I might show you."

"I'm not being a good girl *until* you show me."

"Fine, be a bad one then." Steve grabbed her waist and lifted her. "Ride me." He brought her down.

The new position altered the angle, allowed for deeper penetration. Sensations unfolded, floated out to cover every part of her. Gordie leaned forward, braced her hands on his shoulders and her knees on the bed beside him. She flexed her leg muscles, used them to raise and lower her body on his. On the downward plunge she rotated her hips and ground her clit on his pubic bone.

Gordie took her time. Learned what made him squirm beneath her, what made her gasp above him. There was no frantic rush to reach the top, only a slow, sensual stroll. His hands left her waist, slid up her ribs to cup her breasts. He pinched her nipples between thumb and forefinger and she leaned into the biting touch. Her blood hummed with arousal, rushed to fill tender tissue with molten fire and set her body alight.

Steve used the pressure of his hands to urge her upright and Gordie gasped as his cock slid over new terrain, making her pussy clench and weep. She cupped his hands with hers and together they squeezed her breasts, played with the tips until they were hard knots of need. He tugged his hands from under hers and dragged his fingers over her belly. Her breath caught and her stomach fluttered. Warmth pooled and dripped lower to her sex.

"Don't stop. Keep playing with your breasts. Show me what gives you pleasure."

His words sent a shiver of delight through her and Gordie granted his wish. She tweaked her nipples, pulled them away from her body and twisted. A moan slipped from her throat, the sound deep and gravelly as it vibrated in her ears. She jolted as Steve's finger brushed her clit. The contact sent a dart of fire from the tight bundle of nerves to her core, delivering heat and need.

Her hips rocked, rode his cock in small, sharp thrusts as she concentrated on the wicked swirl of desire skyrocketing inside. Steve continued to ply her clit with skilled fingers. He took her to the edge then backed off only to push her up again. His other hand cupped her ass, his fingers delving between her cheeks to tease the puckered flesh of her anus. She bucked wildly, thrashed back and forth as he pressed harder on the delicate opening.

He touched her in a way no one ever had. Inside and out he knew just what she needed for maximum pleasure. His touch quickened, slowed, sped up again. The varied pace drove her mad. She tried to catch his rhythm but every time she caught on he changed the beat.

"Steve." Gordie gasped for air. "Please. I need."

"Then you shall have." He breached the tight ring of muscle to her back entrance at the same time he applied pressure to her clit and drove his cock up into her. Gordie disintegrated. Stars burst before her eyes as the climax roared through her, dragging every last breath from her lungs and every thought from her mind.

4

GORDIE WOKE to sunshine streaming through the skylight above her. Crystal-clear, blue sky without a cloud in sight filled the large, circular glass roof section. Steve stirred next to her and she turned her head to look at him. Dark stubble covered his chin and cheeks, soot-black eyelashes fanned out over his tan skin and the thick slash of his eyebrows curved over his closed eyes.

She wouldn't call him beautiful, he was too rugged, too large for that. But the very thing that kept him from being handsome made him striking. There was an edge to his attraction, a hard one. Gordie had always found him gorgeous. In high school he'd been the one she wanted to date. All the other girls wanted Brogan or Quinn, even Marcus had pulled his share of clamoring females, but Steve was different.

He dated but not like the others. Rarely did she see him out with a girl more than a few times. In fact she couldn't remember him ever having a serious girlfriend. She certainly hadn't seen him date anyone since she'd come home from medical school. It struck her as strange that a man as appealing and manly as Steve wouldn't date.

"You think too hard, Doc."

Her gaze darted to his, those deep-brown orbs studying her. "I didn't know you were awake."

"I noticed. You wouldn't have been checking me out so thoroughly if you'd known I was."

"I wasn't—"

"Uh-uh." He pressed a finger to her mouth. "No more hiding, Doc."

Gordie sighed. "Fine, I was checking you out." She spoke against his skin, the rough texture catching on her lips as they moved.

"And what did you find that was so distasteful?"

"What? Nothing. Why do you ask that?"

"Your nose was all scrunched up and your lips were puckered as though you'd eaten something sour."

"Oh." She tried to think of something to tell him, anything but what she'd actually been thinking.

"Well? And stop trying to come up with a plausible answer."

"Hey. I wasn't."

"Gordie, what were you thinking about?"

She huffed out a breath. "If you really must know, I was thinking how I hadn't seen you date anyone since I came home and that's not normal."

"Ah. So that wonderful mind of yours was about to come up with reasons why you haven't seen me with anyone."

"Well, no. I hadn't gotten that far yet." She smiled sheepishly. He was right. It would have been the next logical step.

"I'm not sure you're ready for the answer to that, Gordie."

"Why?"

Steve brushed his fingers over her temple, pushed a few

strands of hair back from her face. "You."

"Me? I don't understand."

"I know you don't." He cupped her chin and tilted her mouth toward his for a quick kiss. "Come on. Let's get going. We'll round up the troops and get them out of here so we can have this conversation in private."

"We are in private, why can't you tell me what you mean now?"

"Because I don't want to explain myself right now." Steve rolled over and climbed out of bed.

"What? Just like that, Steve doesn't want to talk so he gets to stay silent but Gordie can't have the same privilege?"

"*Doc.*"

"No. No more hiding goes both ways. I want to know now."

"Fine." He stomped around the bed until he towered over her. "You want to know why I don't date, I'll tell you. From before you married Anthony I wanted you. No one else. But it scared the shit out of me knowing I'd have to turn you. You were human, Doc, and I wasn't even out of my teens. I never touched you because I knew if I did I wouldn't stop and I wasn't sure either of us could handle that back then."

He took a deep breath, dragged his fingers through his hair, making it stick up at all angles. "And then it didn't matter. You were with Anthony."

Oh God. She hadn't known. Probably wouldn't have accepted Anthony's proposal if she had. "Oh, Steve."

"No." He stepped away. "I don't want your pity."

"Pity's the last thing I'm feeling." She sat up, pulled the covers over her bare breasts. "If I feel anything it's sadness— guilt. I never would have agreed to marry Anthony and let him turn me if I'd known how you felt."

Steve stood staring at her, probing with that intense gaze of his. Gordie couldn't stop the anger bubbling inside her. Not at him, never at Steve. At herself for being selfish enough to accept the offer of a friend when she'd known full well it was a one-sided relationship. She'd used Anthony and he'd let her. They were both to blame for so much, but the majority of shame fell on her.

"He'd still be alive if I hadn't been so selfish." She lowered her head. "Hadn't wanted desperately to be like everyone else."

"No. If we're laying down guilt then I'm to blame for not coming to you with how I felt. If I hadn't been a coward..."

Gordie's head snapped up and she stared at Steve. "That's ridiculous."

"Yes, it is." He reached for her hand, entwined their fingers. "So is blaming yourself for Anthony's death. No one could have stopped the accident. And you and I know that even if you hadn't been married you both would have been going on that trip. The crash would still have happened."

She heard his words, knew he was right but her heart wouldn't believe it. Not when she'd spent years living with the heavy weight of guilt over Anthony's death. Gordie tried to smile, her lips trembling as she made the effort to reassure him. "I know you're right but it's hard to accept when I've made so many life-altering mistakes."

Voices coming from the other side of the door drew their attention. Gordie could hear Kat clear as a bell yelling she'd have breakfast on the table in thirty minutes. She smiled. Her sister might be loud, pushy and a pain in the ass, but Gordie loved her to pieces and had from the minute she'd been born.

"Sounds like everyone is up," Gordie said.

"If they weren't, they are now. Does Kat have a volume switch?"

Gordie laughed. "Not that we've ever found. When she was little, Mom always threatened to gag her if she couldn't be quiet."

"Mmm, that might work." Steve tugged on her hand. "Come on, let's get showered and dressed. We've got a long day ahead of us and the sooner we get started the sooner we'll get finished."

"I've got nothing to wear." Gordie let him pull her to her feet but held onto the sheet. She had to let it go when her feet got tangled up. If it wasn't for Steve's grip she would have fallen on her face.

"You can borrow something of mine and change when we get to your house. You can pack enough clothes to last until you open the clinic back up in the New Year while we're there." He pulled her behind him as he headed for the bathroom. "We'll worry about moving all your stuff later."

Gordie stumbled. "My stuff?"

"Yeah, clothes, furniture, any knickknacks you want to keep, that sort of thing."

"Furniture?"

Steve twisted the tap in the shower and turned to face her. "Doc, did you think you wouldn't be moving in with me now?"

"Moving in?"

He shook his head. "I'm going to assume you're still shaken up after yesterday because I know you're smarter than this, Doc. I want you here, in my house. If you want to wait until your mom and Doctor Monroe can get back to Whispering Springs to get married we can, but that's the only thing we're going to wait for."

"Oh." They were getting married? The words rolled around her head. They felt comfortable and Gordie felt a fluttering in her belly. *Married to Steve.* The idea thrilled her. "Okay."

A sexy smile curled one side of his mouth. "Back to agreeable Doc?"

Gordie couldn't help it. She grinned. "Oh yeah, definitely agreeable."

Pushing up onto her toes, she wrapped her arms around his neck and pulled his mouth down to meet hers. The kiss went on and on. By the time they pulled apart, both were breathless and steam filled the space around them. Hot and wet, inside and out, Gordie tried to remember what they were doing.

"Damn, woman. You trying to scramble my brains?" Steve licked his lips and a shiver snaked down her spine.

She laughed. "If I am, I can't remember why."

Steve's arms tightened around her waist and he lifted her against him. He stepped back, maneuvering them both under the shower. Warm water cascaded down, wetting her hair and splashing into her eyes. She shut her eyelids and tilted her head back to let the water flow over her face. The air surrounding them was charged with heat, the steamy enclosure trapping the sexual energy as easily as Steve clasped her body to his.

He lowered her to her feet. Her skin sliding along his sent sparks of desire shooting through her. His arms loosened and she turned in his embrace to reach for the soap. Gordie lathered her hands before dropping the bar back in the holder and spinning back to run her soapy fingers all over Steve's chest.

She left no area untouched, took extra care to be sure she cleaned every inch of his broad torso. Her insides swirled with desire, touching his muscular physique ramped up her arousal with each stroke of a finger. She moved on to his shoulders.

The wide expanse reminded her of just how big he was. At six feet six inches, Steve was easily the tallest man she'd ever met. It made her feel small and delicate—feminine. She wasn't small for a woman, a little above average at five feet six, but he was a full foot taller than her and yet they fit together so well. Gordie stretched to rake her hands up and around his neck. He bent forward, giving her better access and she curled her fingertips into his muscles, used gentle pressure to work out the knots.

"Man that feels good."

"You're all tense."

Steve chuckled. "I'm in the shower naked with *you*. Believe me when I say the tension you're feeling is the good kind."

"Oh." Gordie stood on her toes and ran her fingers over his scalp. Her body brushed against his, her breasts pressed into his chest and her nipples pebbled as his coarse hair abraded them. She shivered.

"Gordie." Her name was a whispered breath seconds before his head lowered and his mouth took hers.

He thrust his tongue between her lips, probed inside with bold strokes and carnal demands. Heat swirled deep in her belly, her pussy weeping with a demand of its own. She moaned into his mouth, drove her tongue forward to tangle with his. Her fingernails dug into his scalp as she held him to her and took as much as she surrendered.

The kiss was a challenge, a duel. A meshing of mouths designed to bring each of them to their knees. Only it made them stronger. Fueled their desire until the flames threatened to consume them both. His hands cupped her ass, pulled her tighter to him and brought their pelvises together in a lock as old as time. Gordie lifted her legs and wrapped them around his hips. They both moaned when her pussy rubbed against his cock.

He tore his mouth from hers. "Put me inside you," he growled.

"Yes." She reached between them as Steve used his grip on her behind to lift her away from his body. Her fingers encircled his length and held him in place as he pulled her back against him. Slick folds opened, welcomed him with grasping contractions as she sank down his length—each ripple firing nerve endings like a match to a fuse. Gordie buried her face in his neck and moaned.

Steve's grip on her ass tightened and he worked his fingers closer to where his body joined hers, teasing sensitive flesh with skill. He knew just where to touch, when to touch, to drive her crazy. She rocked her hips, tried to get him to move inside her but he continued to tease her while holding her snug against him. Desperate for more, she tangled her fingers in his hair and pulled.

"Move, dammit."

"No." His breath puffed in her ear and he nipped at her lobe with his teeth. "Want. To. Last."

Gordie could hear his teeth grind as he clenched his jaw in an obvious effort for control. But she wanted none of that. She wanted hot and wild. Needed it with razor-sharp edges. With a growl, she sank her teeth into his shoulder. He jerked, his cock sliding over her swollen walls.

"*Yes.*"

She tugged on his hair, licked at the slope of skin that led from his shoulder to his neck and worked her pelvic floor muscles in a punishing wave of catch and release. His control snapped with the click of his jaw. One breath he was still and the next he was powering in and out of her pussy like a man possessed. Gordie let go of his hair to wrap her arms around his neck and hold on.

Over and over he drove into her. Hard. Fast. She bounced against him with the force of his thrusts, her clit grinding on his body with every lunge. Her pussy clenched with the first of many convulsions as her orgasm roared through her and into him. Gordie's hips bucked and thrashed as Steve's name fell from her lips and her name burst from his. They came together in a rush, the ride over before it had barely begun.

Gasping for air, she held on to him as he leaned on the wall behind them and slowly slid to the floor. She straddled his hips, his cock still buried and pulsing inside her. Cold water poured down over them but she didn't care. Nothing could take away the bliss coursing through her veins.

"Water's cold. We have to get out before we turn into icicles." Steve let her go to reach up and switch the shower off. He put his arm back around her and squeezed. "Just need a minute to catch my breath."

"When you're done hunting yours, can you chase down mine?" she murmured into his neck.

His chest vibrated with a chuckle, the tremors tickled her nipples and sent tiny shards of pleasure blasting out in all directions. A shudder raked through her from head to toes.

"You're getting cold."

He surged to his feet, his softened cock slipping from her body as he stood. Her pussy clenched with loss, a hollow ache filling her core where his warmth had been. Steve placed her on her feet and enveloped her in a warm towel. Goose bumps sprang up along her skin as he rubbed her down. The soft terrycloth gently absorbed every last droplet of water. Banging on the bathroom door startled them.

"Come on, you two, breakfast is ready," Kat yelled.

"We'll be right out," Steve answered.

They waited until they heard the bedroom door close behind Kat before venturing out of the bathroom. Steve tossed a clean t-shirt and sweatpants on the bed for her and Gordie quickly pulled them on. The first thing she planned to do when she got to her house was dress in some of her own clothes. She shivered with the thought of what she might find this time when she unlocked her front door.

"Hey." Steve stepped up behind her, ran his hands from her elbows to her shoulders and back again. "It'll be fine. I'll be with you when you go inside so there's nothing to worry about."

She knew he would do his best to protect her from any danger, but he couldn't stop the dread eating at her gut. Her biggest fear was that Dale was right. The game had changed and now no one was safe from Marcus' madness.

STEVE TURNED Doc to face him and bent his knees to bring their eyes level. "I promise he won't hurt you again."

"You can't promise that, Steve. We have no idea what he'll do or when. All we can do is take precautions and be prepared."

"He won't hurt you." Steve's gut churned. The idea of anything happening to Doc burned in his chest and tasted foul on his tongue. He pulled her close, tucked her head under his chin and breathed her in.

She relaxed and cuddled into him. He knew she was right, he couldn't promise Marcus wouldn't hurt her but he'd be damned if he didn't do everything he could to protect her. He'd start with moving her into his house permanently. After they'd had something to eat and plowed their way to town. Steve hoped their trip to her place was uneventful but he didn't discount the buzz of his instincts. There was no way he would let her out of his sight until they'd driven back up the mountain and locked the front door behind them.

"Come on, let's eat." He dropped a kiss on the top of her head and released her. Curling his hand around hers, he pulled her with him out of the room and toward the noise coming from the other end of the house.

When they reached the dining room, everyone was already there and before he could say a word Doc sprinted across the room.

"Tatum."

The two women embraced before Doc pushed Tatum to arm's length and glanced down at her pregnant belly.

"Yeah, we're growing a little bigger than expected."

"A little? What have you got in there, triplets?"

Tatum laughed. "No, just your run-of-the-mill, everyday twins."

"Have you been taking your vitamins? Eating right? Getting plenty of rest?"

"Yes, yes, yes." Tatum laughed.

"Wait. When did you get here? How did you get here?"

"Sit down, my back is killing me." Tatum took her seat again. "We'll catch up while we eat. I'm starving."

Steve pulled out a chair for Doc, sliding it back in as she sat. He took the chair next to her and began loading her plate and his with scrambled eggs, hash browns, sausages and bacon. Kat passed him the coffeepot and he filled both their mugs.

"Hey, I can't eat all this," Doc complained.

"Try to put a dent in it," he said.

"I'll eat whatever you don't." Tatum patted her protruding belly. "Bottomless stomach."

"There's plenty of food, you don't have to eat off Gordie's plate." Kat offered the platter of bacon to Tatum.

"Oh, don't worry." Tatum scooped up a pile of crispy strips. "I'll eat this *and* hers."

"Don't eat too much. I'd hate for you to throw up in my car on the way back to town," Dale said.

"Who said I'm traveling with you?"

Dale stared across the table at Tatum. Steve waited for the sheriff to back down like he had the night before but this time it was Tatum's turn to give in.

"Fine. But I'm eating as much as I want. I haven't chucked since the first month of my pregnancy and I don't plan on starting again now."

He thought it best to deflect any more discussion of vomiting at the breakfast table. "I'll take the plow out as soon as we've eaten. It won't take long to get to town. Anyone take a look this morning to see how deep the snow is?"

"Yeah, we got about a foot. Not much considering how hard it was coming down when we went to bed," Brogan said as he reached for the coffeepot.

"Only a foot?" Steve had expected much more than that.

"If we all follow you down the mountain we shouldn't have any problems. Once you've plowed, our snow tires and chains should handle the road easily." Quinn pushed back his chair and picked up his plate. "Are we heading to the clinic or Doc's house first?"

"Doc's. I want to get in and out of there as quickly as possible and I didn't think we needed to go back to the clinic," Steve said between bites of food.

"Someone will have to pull my car out of the ditch," Tatum mumbled around a mouthful.

"Your car? Why is your car in a ditch?" Gordie asked.

"I slid on some ice down the road a bit last night, had to walk the rest of the way." Tatum shoveled food into her mouth as if she hadn't eaten in months.

"You what?" Gordie pushed her chair back and stood. "Get up. I want to check you over."

"Relax, Doc, I did some checking of my own and I'm good."

"You can't examine yourself." Doc's hands went to her hips.

Steve bit the inside of his cheek to hold in the chuckle at Doc's attempt to give Tatum a stern look. The other woman raised one eyebrow and continued to eat breakfast. He'd come to the conclusion that Tatum did whatever the hell she wanted and you either got in line with her or bashed your head on an invisible brick wall.

"Eat some more and then I'll let you take a look at us, Doc."

Tatum aimed her fork at Gordie's plate. "If you wait too long I'll snatch that bacon up."

He watched Doc struggle to decide what to do. That mind of hers was trying to work out whether it was worth arguing. With a sigh, she sat back down and Steve patted her leg. She glanced at him and smiled. Warmth flowed through him, centered in his chest and he leaned over to drop a peck on her lips.

"Eat up. You can check Tatum's okay while I get the plow ready to go."

"Honestly, Doc, I'm fine. I was tired from the walk but no bumps or bruises mar this tub of a body."

"You weren't hurt in the crash?"

"Crash is far too severe a word to use for the slide that put me in the ditch. That old tank of mine just rolled to a stop nose down. It was the best stop I've ever made and I wasn't even in control."

"Maybe that's why?" Dale said.

Steve glanced across the table at his friend. The man had wrinkles on his forehead and his lips were stretched in a thin line as he stared at Tatum. Tension vibrated between them, the air crackling with some fight he wasn't privy to.

"Yes, you've made yourself clear about your opinion of my driving, Sheriff."

Everyone was silent. No one breathed as the two of them faced off. He didn't have a clue what was going on or why and he really didn't have time to worry about it. To his surprise, Tatum was the first to break their death stare.

"Thanks for a great breakfast, Kat." Tatum pushed her chair back and stood. "When you're ready, Doc, I'll be in the room I shared with Kat."

One by one his friends got up and followed Tatum to the

kitchen with their plates. As he and Doc had been the last to sit down they were still eating when everyone else had gone.

"What's going on with Dale and Tatum?" he asked.

"I have no idea."

"But you knew she was coming back to the mountains."

"Yeah, she rang me early last month and asked if I was still looking for a nurse to help out part-time at the clinic." Doc took a sip of coffee. "It's hard to get anyone on account of them needing to be coyote so I told her anytime she turned up she had a job."

"Obviously she accepted."

"She told me she'd start mid-January."

"Did she also tell you she was pregnant?"

"Yes. Said she wanted to bring her babies into the world at home."

"What about the father? And it's not like this has been home for her in years."

"I don't know, Steve. All I know is I'd give my right arm for some help at the clinic and she's just what I'd wish for. I remember her coming to the clinic when Dad was still there. She had to be about ten and even then she knew she wanted to be a nurse."

"Seems strange that she'd stay away for so long and suddenly come back. Babies aside, it just doesn't seem right."

"I guess, but then look at Dale. He came back out of the blue and look how well that worked out."

"Yeah, it was a good thing for the pack."

"This will be too."

"I hope so."

They finished their meal in silence and Steve stacked their plates and mugs. He stood. "You go take a look at Tatum. I know you were thinking about it the whole time you ate breakfast."

She stood beside him and smiled. "Thanks. I am worried, especially now I know she drove her car into a ditch last night."

He kissed her forehead. "Go, I'll clear these away and meet you in the garage when you're done."

Steve found Kat alone in the kitchen loading the dishwasher and as much as he didn't want to have a conversation with her about her sister, he figured it was unavoidable and probably best to get it over and done with. He didn't need to start talking. She fired a question at him before he'd taken three steps into the room.

"You going to let her run you around for the next few years or will you man up and marry her?" She kept her back to him and didn't stop what she was doing.

He walked over to the sink and rinsed the plates and cups, handing them to her to stack in the dishwasher. When he was done he turned and leaned back against the counter, waited for her to look at him.

Kat put the final dish in the machine and straightened. She looked at him but before he could say a word she spoke again.

"I'm preaching to the choir, aren't I?" She sighed.

Steve smiled. "Yeah."

"She can't really give you the runaround now though, can she? I mean it's not like she can change what you did yesterday and everyone is going to smell you on her so whether she likes it or not she'll have to own up to it."

"I think she will. You know what Doc's like, once she makes up her mind it's full steam ahead."

"I can't believe she didn't say anything about that fucking dress."

The subject change threw him for a second but he soon caught up with her. "Did you notice anything odd at the house?"

"No. The only difference to any other night we've shared

dinner was her wanting me to stay over."

"Nothing about the house seemed off? What about Doc?"

"She was a little tense but then she always is this time of year so I didn't think too much of it. In fact that's what I put her asking me to sleep there down to." Kat shrugged. "Figured she just wanted to know she wasn't alone."

He rubbed the back of his neck. "I'm moving her in here as of yesterday. We'll collect essentials today and leave the house locked up until after New Year or when your parents arrive, whichever comes first. Maybe you should think about staying out here with us."

"I was planning to spend the next week with Wendy. She isn't going home for Christmas this year and with Mom and Dad arriving sometime before New Year's Eve, I think it best I stay in town."

"You and Wendy could come out here."

Kat placed a hand on his arm. "Steve, I know you're just being the gentlemen you are but you don't really want me and Wendy underfoot for the next week. Besides, I think you and Gordie deserve to have this next week locked away in this house on the mountain. So I will gracefully consider your offer but regretfully decline it."

Steve laughed. "Was I that obvious?"

"No, but the sparks that fly between you two are sure to singe my hair if I stand too close." She grinned. "Go get the plow ready so we can get this show on the road."

He wasn't sure which one of them was more surprised when he pulled her into his arms for a hug. Kat remained stiff for a second before giving him one quick squeeze and breaking free.

"I'm glad you two finally got together. Gordie deserves to be happy and you're the one man I know who'll make sure she will be."

She strode from the room before he could comment. His chest tightened and his heart beat hard against his sternum. That Kat thought he was good for Doc pleased him way more than he thought it should. He'd never considered anyone's opinion important. The only person he'd ever set out to please was Doc and he'd screwed that up in so many ways he'd often thought he didn't deserve her. But Kat's faith in him made him feel worthy and Steve would do everything in his power to prove her right.

Steve headed for the garage. He found Brogan, Quinn and Dale already there, struggling to fit the snow plow to the front of his truck. Glancing through the open roller door he saw they'd already shoveled the driveway and turn-around so he could get the truck out.

"How the fuck does this thing go on?" Brogan asked.

"With great difficulty, but it shouldn't be too hard with all of us here. Normally it's just me that fits it," Steve said.

"Why isn't it on already? You usually have this thing on from late November or early December." Quinn stood straight. "I can't get that thing to lock in."

"We haven't had as much snow this year." Steve bent down to adjust a bracket on the front of his truck. "There, that should do it."

They worked together and quickly had the single-blade plow fitted for the trip to town. He'd leave it on now, until late February, that way he'd be able to get to and from town without much trouble. Since he'd moved into his house he no longer had direct access to the town plow, it was kept in a storage shed behind the community center and Harry was now in charge of clearing the main streets in Whispering Springs.

"Ready?" Dale asked.

"As I'll ever be," Steve answered.

"We'll all go to Doc's house. The women can help her get

some things together to bring back here and we'll take a look around," Brogan said.

"Thanks."

"Don't thank me, Steve. I should have killed the bastard when we caught him. Instead I did the right thing and had him exiled." Brogan's fists clenched at his sides.

"You weren't the only one who had your hands on him that day. And remember I didn't rip his throat out even though I knew what had happened to Doc up here last May." Steve had almost given in to the need to hurt Marcus that day, but he hadn't.

"Water under the bridge. What if's will eat you alive if you let them, best to move on and learn from your mistakes." Dale walked over to the door to the house. "I'll tell the women we're ready to go whenever they are."

"So what's going on between our sheriff and Tatum?" Quinn asked.

"No idea. I asked Doc before and she's as clueless as I am," Steve said.

"She's a tough little thing, stood up to him without batting an eyelid." Brogan pulled his keys out of his pocket. "Never thought I'd see that. Most run a mile and it's not his size that frightens people, it's the *don't come near me* vibe he gives off."

"Yeah, I know what you mean. He's been like that all his life but it's worse since he returned from the city," Quinn added.

Steve could understand that. The thought of living in the city for years put him in a bad mood, never mind actually living there. "The city will do that to you."

"Not sure it was the city or what happened in it that made him worse." Quinn headed for the driveway. "I'm gonna warm up my truck, tell Rowan that's where I am when she finally gets her ass in gear."

"Hey, my ass is in gear." Rowan stepped out of the house into the garage. "Don't go getting all smart mouthed or Santa won't bring you any presents."

Brogan laughed. "Santa isn't likely to bring Quinn anything but coal in his sack. He's got bad boy ticks tallied up until eternity."

"Like you're any better." Rowan swatted her brother on the arm as she walked past.

"Hey." Brogan cradled his arm against his chest.

"Are those two at it again?" El asked.

"Quinn started it." Brogan and Rowan spoke together.

Quinn rolled his eyes and turned to head outside. "I'm leaving now, Rowan."

"I'm coming, I'm coming." She jogged after him.

"Come on, let's get this show on the road." Brogan offered his hand to El and led her from the garage.

Everyone else filed out of the house and Steve locked the door. Dale escorted Tatum with a hand on her elbow out to his squad car and Kat jumped in the back of Brogan's truck, which left him and Doc.

"Kat could have come with us," he said.

"I think she wanted to talk to Brogan about something."

"Oh?"

"Yeah, something about the new guide starting next year. She's supposed to do some training with him, I think. I can't remember exactly what she told me."

He helped Gordie into the truck and shut the door. Jumping over the plow, he skirted the front end and got in the driver's seat. In no time he'd reversed out and turned around. Steve drove through the unshoveled side of his driveway to the road. One by one the other vehicles fell in behind him and they headed for town.

5

GORDIE JUMPED from Steve's truck when he pulled up to the curb in front of her childhood home. The place looked quiet, but a raw nerve twitched deep in her belly. She wasn't sure what it was but something felt wrong. Very wrong. Her instincts screamed run but she was done with running from Marcus and the fear he'd made her live with for months.

Steve stepped up beside her and grabbed her hand, entwining their fingers. He waited without saying a word while the others pulled up one car at a time and came to join them on the sidewalk. There wasn't as much snow on the ground here as there had been higher up the mountain at Steve's place, but there was enough to know nobody had walked up to the house from the street.

"Ready?" Steve gave her hand a gentle squeeze.

She sucked in a deep breath and blew it out through her mouth. "Yep. Let's do this."

They walked up the snow-covered path, their shoes sinking into the iced-over top with ease. Gordie wore a pair of boots Steve had loaned her, they were too big and her toes kept bashing into the steel-capped tips as her feet slid forward with each step. She'd have bruises if she didn't get out of them soon. Good thing hers were on the other side of that door.

Gordie froze on the bottom step. She hadn't even thought about her purse, never mind her keys. "I don't have—"

"Here." Steve held her keys out in his hand.

"Oh. Thank you." She gripped the key ring, reluctant to find the right key to open the front door. What was the warning bell going off in her head all about?

"What's wrong?" Dale came up behind them.

She turned her head and saw everyone else waiting back on the footpath. "I'm not sure."

"Want me to go in first?" Dale asked.

Gordie tilted her head and looked up at the second floor windows and stilled. There's no way she'd left her bedroom window open. "Yes." She handed over the keys.

Steve turned her to face him. "I'll go in with Dale. You go wait with the others while we take a look inside, okay?"

She thought about taking the easy way out, just going over and waiting for someone else to deal with whatever mischief Marcus had wrought in her house, but she couldn't do it. "No. I'm coming in with you."

"Doc."

"It's my house, my problem."

"Dale." Steve turned to the other man. "Tell her to wait outside."

"Can't. Technically this isn't an official call, otherwise I would." Dale looked at Gordie. "But if I tell you to move you move, got it?"

She nodded. Gordie might be brave enough to go in with them, but she wasn't about to question the authority of a sheriff who'd spent years on the mean streets of a big city.

"Right, let's go then." Dale walked to the door, key out. "Both of you stay behind me."

Steve shoved her behind him as they entered the house. The stench hit her full in the face like a brick wall. It was worse than a litter box. Gordie pinched her nose and breathed through her mouth until she got in the rhythm of breathing through her mouth only. Puddles of yellow fluid lined the walls and floor in the foyer and explained where the smell came from.

"Fuck." Steve pulled her with him into the living room. "I take it you didn't leave the place like that yesterday morning?"

"You take it right." Gordie quickly scanned the room. "There's none in here."

"No, it appears to just be in the entrance." Dale strode toward the dining area.

Gordie held tight to Steve's hand as they followed the sheriff through her house. There was another "marking of territory" section at her back door but nothing else on the lower level appeared to have been touched. At the stairs she took a deep breath through her mouth and tried to calm the nerves jumping around inside her. She knew whatever they found upstairs would be above and beyond the downstairs damage.

Kat's childhood bedroom was trashed. The furniture had been overturned and the bedding ripped from the bed. Gordie wanted to cry at the sight of her sister's prized collection of porcelain dolls—the clothes were in tatters and their pretty, painted faces smashed to smithereens.

"Jesus." Steve tugged on her hand. "Don't touch anything. Dale might be able to get fingerprints."

"I'll want photos too before you move anything, Gordie," Dale said.

She nodded and spun on her heel to leave the room but stopped when she saw the wall behind her. Gordie's chest ached when all the air was sucked from her lungs. Painted on the wall, in crude preschool skill, was a coyote, his eyes glowed un-naturally yellow, saliva dripped from its jaws and clamped between wicked-looking teeth was a cat. It didn't take a genius to work out what the message was.

"Get her off the street." Gordie took off at a run, a scream tearing from her throat. "*Kat!*"

"Gordie, wait."

She could hear Steve's boots hitting the hardwood flooring as he raced after her, but she couldn't stop. Had to reach Kat before anything happened. Her feet slid in the borrowed boots and she stumbled on the staircase. A hand gripped her forearm, fingers dug into her soft flesh and sent shards of pain slicing through her elbow and wrist. Gordie felt herself spin midair, her footing gone from underneath her completely but instead of landing on hard, wooden treads she slammed into the hot, hard wall of Steve's chest.

He held her close and they went down together. His body cushioned their fall and air expelled from his lungs as his back hit the stairs with a thud. Steve groaned in pain and Gordie had visions of snapping vertebrae before her breasts crushed against his ribs, sucking all breath from her. The front door burst open beneath them. Footfalls pounded the stairs above and below them, but she couldn't get past the look of agony on Steve's face.

Stars danced in her vision and pain lanced her chest. Gordie tried to suck in air, tried to move her arms and legs to get off him but nothing wanted to work properly. Her ears filled with a strange humming sound that she tried to shake loose but it didn't stop. Finally her lungs worked, lifesaving oxygen flowed through her veins bringing with it vital feeling and function.

She planted her hands on the step beside Steve's shoulders

and pushed to lift her weight off him. He still hadn't spoken and the color of his skin was making her feel sick. She scrambled up, moved to the side and began to check his limbs for breakage.

"Where does it hurt? Can you feel your toes? Talk to me, Steve." She rambled on as she cleared one section of his body after another of any injury.

Steve tried to say something and she bent forward to listen but couldn't make out the words. She checked his pupils. Both reacted normally and Gordie breathed a sigh of relief that he didn't appear to have banged his head in the fall. His color was returning along with a harsh breath he dragged in through clenched teeth.

"Don't try to move. Let me check the rest of you." Gordie ran her hands under his head and another sigh left her chest when she found no lumps.

"Okay," he panted. "Catch. Breath."

"What?"

"Winded."

"Are you sure?"

He nodded.

"Okay, everyone back, give him room." She thrust out her hands to ward everyone off without taking her eyes off Steve's.

"I'm okay, Doc. You can relax now."

Relax? They just tumbled down half a flight of stairs and he wanted her to relax? "Not going to happen until you get up and walk and talk normally."

"Give me a second."

"Here, let me help you sit." Dale spoke from above them.

Dale shoved his hands under Steve's shoulders and lifted. Steve groaned but didn't change color or faint. That was a win as far as she was concerned. Gordie moved aside and helped him sit with an arm around his waist. He leaned in against her and she pushed back to keep them both from falling into everyone crammed onto the steps below them.

"What happened? Why were you screaming my name at the top of your lungs?" Kat asked.

Oh God. She'd forgotten about that. Gordie looked at her sister but couldn't come up with the words to explain.

"You old room is trashed and there's a nasty message on one of the walls," Dale told everyone.

Kat raised one eyebrow. "Really? What about the rest of the house?"

"Downstairs is clean except for the piss at the front and back doors. We only got as far as your room when Gordie panicked about you being out on the street."

"Let's check the rest of the house," Brogan said.

"Not without me you're not." Steve tried to stand.

"Hey, you can't get up yet." Gordie tightened her arm around him but only succeeded in getting pulled to her feet with him. "Okay, you can."

"I told you I was fine, just had the wind knocked out of me," he reassured her.

"At least let me check you over first."

"The only thing you're going to find is a few bruises. Honestly, Doc, I'm fine."

She wanted to believe him with every fiber of her being but her heart and her mind wanted proof before he did anything. Gordie checked his eyes again and found no change, just that penetrating gaze of his. He seemed all right so she conceded, but she'd be watching him closely for a while.

"Okay, but any dizziness or numbness or pain you tell me straight away."

"Yes, Doc." He grinned and leaned down to drop a kiss on her mouth. "Thank you for caring."

Gordie's cheeks burned. Everyone stood around them and

even though they all knew she and Steve were together now she couldn't help the blush that stole over her skin.

Dale cleared his throat. "Let's get the rest of the upstairs looked at and then I can take some photos and dust for fingerprints."

"What good will that do? It's not like we don't know who's behind it," Kat said.

"We might know but we need proof because this time he's not getting exiled. I want him locked up," Dale said.

"How will you manage that seeing how he's not human?" El asked from over Brogan's shoulder.

"There are some jails that are shifter friendly." Dale grinned.

"So some humans know about shifters?"

"No, but there are shifters who live among humans and a few are in the correctional services so we have options when it comes to shifters who break the law. In the old days we'd have had to kill them," Dale explained.

"Oh." El wrapped her arms around Brogan's waist. "That's just horrible."

"It's the way it was, but there's been a lot of changes over the years and being able to lock up criminals whether they're human or not is just one of them." Dale turned and headed back up the stairs.

Gordie kept her arm around Steve's waist and walked beside him. He didn't need her support to stay upright but she needed to feel his warmth to reminder her he was fine.

STEVE LET Doc hold him steady. He could walk without her help but after seeing her trip on the stairs and the vision of her hitting bottom that had splashed across his mind in the split second before he'd caught her made him need her touch. She tucked nicely under his arm and he enjoyed the feel of her beside him.

They stopped at the door to Kat's room and everyone took a look inside. Kat whistled and then turned a shade lighter when she got a good look at the painting. She studied it for ages, stepped closer and touched the paint.

"It's dry and if I'm right it's paint like the sort we used in art class back in high school," Kat told them.

Doc reached out a hand and he let her go so the two sisters could hug. It was a brief squeeze and he soon found Doc cuddled back into his side.

"Okay, let's keep going," Doc said.

The bathroom was undisturbed, the tiled expanse clean and tidy. Steve and Doc followed Dale as he made his way along the hallway. Another door revealed a spare room furnished as a home office. This room looked worse than Kat's bedroom.

"Damn. That's a lot of paperwork," Quinn said.

"Yeah, it's the DNA records for my research on the coyote gene. It's not the first time I've found my papers trashed like this but at least it won't set me back months like the first time," Doc said.

"No? Why not?" Steve asked.

"I started keeping a computer record after the first break-in." Dale held up a shattered piece of her hard drive. "And I keep a copy of all my files at an offsite file storage company so my research is safe."

"Good. I doubt there's anything in here you can salvage," Dale said.

There were two rooms left and Steve turned to Doc. "Which one?"

"Mom and Dad's first. I have no doubt mine will be the worst so we'll save it for last."

Doctor and Mrs. Monroe's room was untouched. Like the bathroom not one thing had been moved, it was like the Monroes had gotten up this morning instead of months ago when they'd taken off on their latest cross-country adventure.

"Anyone else find it bizarre that this room is untouched?" Quinn asked.

"No. Downstairs is the same." Dale turned to leave the room. "He's not wasting energy on what won't get a reaction."

Damn, Dale was right. Everything that had been trashed caused an emotional reaction. Marcus was playing mind games with them. It wasn't just about fear either, the way he'd smashed Kat's doll collection held anger but was designed to provoke pain. And the painting, well that had everything to do with menacing Doc. He wanted her to worry about her sister, to fear for her well-being and the dolls played into that too. In his twisted way Marcus was letting Doc know he'd hurt her sister next.

Kat stood next to Dale as he opened the door to Doc's bedroom. All color drained from her face and she swayed.

"Dale." Steve broke his hold on Doc and lunged for her sister but Dale spun in time to catch her and lower her to the floor.

Doc dropped to her knees next to them and patted her sister's cheek. "Come on, Kat, don't faint on me. You're tougher than that."

Kat's eyes fluttered. "Jesus Christ. Steve, don't let them see."

Steve had no idea what she was talking about until he heard Rowan's cry of anguish. He turned and looked past Dale into Doc's room. "Fuck."

Quinn pulled Rowan into his arms and Brogan held El

back away from the door. Steve got to his feet and quickly closed the door. He turned back to the group. "Take everyone downstairs. Doc and Dale stay here."

"Why? What's in there?" El's voice wobbled.

"I don't know and I don't care at the moment. Let's go down and wait for them to join us." Brogan steered her away down the hall.

Tatum and Dale helped Kat to her feet. She'd regained her color and her eyes sparked with heat of the angry kind. Linking her arm with Tatum, they followed the others. Quinn remained with a crying Rowan in his arms. Steve looked at his friend and neither of them had to speak to know what the other was thinking. Marcus would pay for this.

"We won't be long," Steve told him.

Quinn nodded and led Rowan away.

"What the hell is in that room, Steve?" Doc stood beside him. "What could be bad enough for Kat to almost pass out and to send Rowan, who has to be one of the toughest women I know, into a fit of tears?"

He turned to Dale. "One on either side of her?"

Dale nodded and together they bracketed Doc. Steve took a deep breath and cupped her elbow in his palm before opening the door. She surprised him, there was no gasp, no cry, nothing. Until the shaking started. Small tremors that turned into bone-rattling vibrations in seconds.

"Is that what I think it is?" she whispered.

"Yeah, if you think that's Rowan's wedding dress covered in blood."

"Oh God." She brought a trembling hand up to cover her mouth. "Wait, that's not just Rowan's dress."

Steve was unprepared for her to move so she got halfway across the room before he caught up with her. "What do you mean?"

She stood beside the bed gazing down at the red and white mess. Rowan's dress lay draped over the footboard and now that he was closer he could see what Doc was talking about. "El's dress, but whose is the other one?"

"My mother's." She reached out a hand but Dale grabbed it before she could touch anything.

"No, don't touch."

"Come on, we've seen enough. Let Dale do his job."

"I'm calling the station. I need a couple of men over here. Will you let them in and show them upstairs when they get here, Steve?" Dale had his phone to his ear already.

"Sure." Steve ushered Doc from the room.

"I know nothing Marcus has done makes sense but I can't help but wonder about the significance of the dresses. Regardless of his craziness there always seems to be a subliminal message in everything he does," Doc said.

"The message in Kat's room is clear, he's telling you he'll hurt her like the dolls. But I don't have a clue what the message in your room is. The one in your office is clear. Stop researching but why?"

"Stop researching?" She paused and looked at him. "I never made that connection."

"What did you think it was?"

"Just willful mischief."

"No, it's clear to me he's trying to destroy the research you've done so far, which means you'd either start again or give up."

"I'd never give up. What I'm doing will help generations to come."

"What exactly are you doing?"

"I'm tracking skills and bloodlines. Trying to work out if the coyote gene is thinned by breeding with humans or if there's no change to the DNA's strength."

"Found anything yet?"

"Yes, actually. The gene isn't diluted at all. And those that are turned may start with slightly less potent coyote traits but they grow stronger over the years. Depending on how young the individual is when they're turned, they could end up just as strong as a pure-bred coyote shifter."

"How would any of this affect Marcus?"

"I don't know. It was his father that was anti half-bloods and non-bloods but then the apple doesn't fall far from the tree."

"I think you could be right there. Malcolm was insane and it seems Marcus is following right in his footsteps." He slung his arm around her shoulders. "Come on, let's go meet the cavalry."

THEY'D REACHED the bottom step when a knock sounded on the front door. Gordie let Steve answer it, more than happy to allow him to take control for now. Suddenly exhausted, she leaned on the railing for the stairs. She wasn't touching any walls in the foyer. She nodded at the two deputies when they came inside.

"The Sheriff wants us to photograph the downstairs damage before going up, said you'd show us where, Mr. McKenna," the older of the two spoke.

"Here, and beside the back door through the kitchen. Someone has marked territory. Give us a yell when we can clean it up."

"Will do, Mr. McKenna."

Steve walked over and pulled her into his arms. The warmth radiating from his body helped remove the chill that had settled in her bones since she'd seen her room. She didn't want to remember those dresses covered in blood but the image was burned onto her memory like the ink of a tattoo. Gordie sighed and leaned into him.

"I'm not going to promise everything will be okay but I will guarantee I'll be standing beside you no matter what happens," he murmured in her ear, his lips brushing her skin, his breath warm and moist.

Gordie didn't answer him, there didn't seem to be anything but thank you to say and that felt like too little. She wrapped her arms around his waist and raising her head, stood on tippy toes. Her mouth met his in a quick peck. "It seems like too little but thank you."

"You don't need to thank me, Doc. You know I'd be here regardless of our current relationship standing." He grinned.

"What?"

"We're together."

"I know. So?"

"I've waited most of my life for this moment and with everything going on it's only just sunk in." Steve lifted her off the floor and spun around.

"Put me down."

"No." He stopped spinning and planted his mouth on hers.

This kiss was nothing like the chaste one she'd given him. It was wet and hot. He thrust his tongue through her lips. She opened wider and their tongues tangled, stroked and licked until she was breathless with want. Gordie curled her legs around his hips and pressed her sex to his. Her pussy clenched and moisture coated her panties. Steve groaned into her mouth and bucked his hips.

"Ahem."

She tore her mouth from his. Ragged breaths dragged over her teeth and along her raw throat. Her eyes wide, Gordie stared at Steve. They'd been seconds from taking the kiss to the next level and she'd totally forgotten where they were. Who was with them. There was a house full of people and she was moments away from stripping him bare.

"Sorry to interrupt, but could you show us where else down here needs photographing, please?"

The young deputy ducked his head but not before Gordie noticed the pink tinge on his cheeks. She looked at the other officer to find him staring back with a knowing smile. Her own cheeks flushed with heat, more than was already there from Steve's carnal kisses.

"This way." Steve turned and headed through the living room, Gordie still in his arms.

"Put me down," she whispered.

"No." He kept walking.

They passed everyone sitting at her dining table, mugs of coffee or tea in front of them. Gordie was glad to see her sister had played hostess. Steve stepped into the kitchen and indicated the door to the mudroom.

"In there."

Both men entered the small room but it soon became apparent the space wasn't large enough for the two of them. The older man came back into the kitchen and pulled a notebook from his shirt pocket.

"Got a second to answer some questions?" he asked as he licked the tip of a pen.

"The sheriff was with us when we came in," Steve said.

"Yep. And I'll ask him the same questions after I'm done with you."

Steve set Gordie on her feet. "Sure. Mind if we sit while you ask?"

"In here or out there?" The Deputy nodded at the small table and chairs in the far corner of the kitchen before lifting his chin to indicate the dining room behind them.

"In here." Gordie walked over and pulled out a chair.

"Did you see anyone when you got here?"

"No and the layer of snow on the front walk hadn't been disturbed either," Steve answered.

"Okay, so in your own words talk me through what happened." He sat opposite them, scribbling in his notebook.

Gordie let Steve tell him. She could have done it but she was tired and wasn't sure she wouldn't burst into tears if she had to say what had been done to the upstairs rooms. Resting her head on Steve's shoulder, she closed her eyes and let the sound of his voice soothe her.

She must have dozed off because next thing she knew Steve was lifting her into his arms and carrying her out of the kitchen. He headed upstairs and she tensed. The thought of seeing all that carnage again terrified her.

"It's okay, Kat changed the sheets on your parents' bed. We're just going to have a lie down."

"But—"

"Dale and the deputies are downstairs talking to the others and Kat, Rowan and El have already cleaned up the mess down there." He walked along the hall and she was relieved to see all the doors were shut tight.

"How long have I been asleep?"

"About thirty minutes but you need to rest and you need to freshen up too. Kat is heading over to the café in a few minutes and everyone else will leave when she does." Steve nudged open the door to her mom and dad's room. "Dale said he'd be back later with some more equipment and until then we can't clean up here so I vote we take a nap while we can."

He lowered her to the bed and Gordie was surrounded by the smell of her mother. The bedding was fresh from the cupboard and the scent her mom always sprinkled to stop the linen from smelling moldy permeated every thread. She rubbed her cheek on the pillow and breathed deep. Steve tugged off her borrowed shoes and dropped them to the floor before toeing off his and climbing on the bed behind her.

Gordie snuggled into him, her back to his front, and relaxed. His warmth and the comfort of his arm draped over her waist calmed her in a way nothing in her life ever had. Even with the turmoil rolling around them she felt safe, secure and most of all loved. She probably wouldn't have taken that final step without yesterday's attack and for that she was thankful. He pressed his lips to her neck and a shiver raced over her skin.

"Go to sleep." His arm tightened around her, his hand splayed across her stomach and those talented fingers stroked her flesh in slow, easy circles.

"Mmm." Her eyelids drooped. "This is nice. Don't let go."

He chuckled. "Don't worry, I won't. You'll need a crowbar to remove me from your life now, Doc."

She smiled and drifted off with his heartbeat drumming against her spine.

STEVE STARED at the ceiling above him. Doc had turned and curled into his side about twenty minutes ago. He hadn't slept, couldn't with all the thoughts going round and round in his mind. Then there was the buzz bouncing from nerve ending to nerve ending currently making his coyote sit up. His instincts were screaming the shit was going to hit the fan. The question was what fan and what shit?

Doc stirred, mumbled something in her sleep and he pulled her closer, held her tighter. He figured they wouldn't be heading back up the mountain today. They would need to clean up once Dale gave them the okay and Steve didn't see that happening before later today. Kat said she'd send some food over from the café for their lunch and knowing her there'd be enough for their dinner plus breakfast and lunch tomorrow.

He should get up. There'd be no sleep for him and besides, he needed to use the bathroom. The sound of a truck pulling up out front made up his mind. Gently as he could, he slipped his arm out from under Doc. She snuggled into the bedding when he tucked it around her. Whatever she dreamed about put a smile on her face and he leaned forward to lightly brush his lips on hers.

Leaving her in that soft, warm bed was hard but he did. With as little noise as possible he picked up his boots, left the room and pulled the door closed behind him. He used the bathroom and had just stepped back into the hall when someone banged on the front door. Taking the stairs two at a time, he made it before whoever it was decided to make more of a racket than they already had. Steve swung the door open to find Dale leaning against the jamb.

"Hey." Steve stepped aside to let him in. "You're back early."

"I figured you'd want to get back up to your place before dark." Dale set down a heavy-looking black case and removed his jacket.

"No, I thought it might be best to stay in town tonight and head back tomorrow."

"Could be. There's supposed to be more snow this evening but not much. It's the big storm due in on Christmas morning that's got me worried." Dale looked at him. "You prepared to get snowed in for a few days up on that mountain of yours?"

"Always."

"Good. Let's grab a coffee before I get started." Dale walked to the kitchen without further invitation.

"Sure, why not?" Steve followed in his socked feet.

"Gordie still sleeping?" Dale was already filling a mug with the pot Kat had made earlier.

"Yes. That can't taste good." He nodded at the coffee in Dale's hand. "I'll put another pot on."

"This is fine. Anything is better than the sludge they try to pass off as coffee at the station. I really need to do something about who makes the coffee over there."

Steve laughed. It might be clichéd but it seemed TV shows were right, cops drank lousy coffee. "Get Kat to deliver some fresh every few hours."

"Now there's a thought." Dale finished and placed his cup in the sink. "Right, down to business."

Before Steve could say a word Dale had left the room. He'd never really been close to Dale when they were younger and since the other man had returned from the city they hadn't strengthened their friendship at all. Steve wasn't even sure if Brogan or Quinn knew him any better, but he wasn't about to let the sheriff's *don't get too close* vibe stop him from watching the man's every move.

He dumped the rest of the coffee from the pot and quickly set about making another one. Doc would want some when she woke up and no doubt they'd all want a few shots of caffeine as the day dragged on. Steve searched cupboards until he came up with coffee grounds and filters. Tossing the old filter in the bin, he dropped in the new one and added the rich-smelling blend. A rinse of the pot in hot water cleaned it enough for him. Once the water was poured in he put the pot on the heated pad under the drip nozzle and pressed the start button.

Heavy footsteps sounded above him. Dale had started in Doc's room. Kat had told him earlier that other than her doll collection there wasn't anything she'd left in her old room that couldn't be replaced easily. Doc's room on the other hand was a completely different story. Those three dresses were irreplaceable. He sucked in a breath and steeled himself to do what was necessary. They'd know in the next few minutes if anything could be done to save the delicate material from the blood soaking it but he wouldn't hold his breath wishing for a miracle.

Steve slipped into his boots and went upstairs to find Dale dusting the windowsill for fingerprints. The room was chilly due to the inch or so of open window. He could see where the lock had been jimmied off so he knew Doc hadn't left it cracked yesterday morning. Standing to the side, he tried to stay out of the way and still be able to see everything the sheriff was doing. When Dale barked an order over his shoulder Steve jumped.

"Bring that bag over here. If you're going to stand there you may as well be useful."

Striding over to the bag that was now open, Steve grabbed the handles and picked it up. He'd been right earlier, the damn thing weighed a ton. "What the hell is in this thing? Rocks?"

Dale laughed. "Rocks would be a lot cheaper."

"Yeah, but then they wouldn't help you get the job done." Steve moved over to the bed and stared at the white-splashed-with-red gowns. "So is this human or animal blood do you think?"

"I'd go with animal but only because I don't want to think about where human blood would come from." Dale finished dusting the window frame and with gloved hands, lowered the bottom section. "I'll be happier when the lab results come in though."

"I guess Marcus has really stepped over the line now."

"He'd stepped over it months ago but coming back after his supposed death has to be the dumbest thing he's ever done."

"So you believed Doc when she said it was him who attacked her yesterday?"

"Didn't you?"

"Well yeah, but there's no proof and you're a cop, you deal in evidence," Steve said.

"Maybe, but you're forgetting I'm also a coyote shifter and instinct is as much a part of my ability to solve crimes as the human skills of gathering information."

"I never thought of that. Guess that makes you better than the average cop."

"Not really, the courts still need hard evidence. Can't just turn up and say he did it because I can smell him all over the victim." Dale grinned.

Steve chuckled. "I can see how that might not work so well."

"Steve?"

He turned to see Doc standing in the doorway. She still wore his clothes and her feet were covered in a pair of his wooly socks. Steve walked over and gathered her in his arms. "I hoped you'd sleep longer."

"Probably best I don't or I won't be able to sleep tonight."

"After I'm through here do you mind if I go over to the clinic and see if I can pick up some prints?" Dale asked.

"No, that's fine. You still have the keys?" She pulled from Steve's embrace.

"Yes ma'am."

"Jeez, don't call me that. Sounds like you're talking to my mother." She grinned.

"Sorry, it's the job. I might not be wearing my uniform, but I'm here in an official capacity," Dale said.

"We'll leave you to finish up, Dale. We're going to get cleaned up so if someone comes by with lunch from Kat, can you let them in?" Steve asked as he ushered Gordie back through the door.

"Sure. I'll be at least another hour in here and then I'll go over Kat's room. Any chance Kat will send enough food for me?"

"Give her a ring and let her know you'll be eating with us," Gordie said. "Although knowing my sister it's probably not necessary."

"Okay."

"Come on, Doc, let's leave the Sheriff to it." Steve pulled her toward the room they'd slept in.

"Where are we going?"

"Back to bed?" he asked hopefully.

Her laughter echoed off the walls. "No way are we doing that in my parents' bed."

"Spoilsport." He pulled her close and whispered in her ear, "Then we'll jump in the shower and I'll help you wash your back."

Steve nipped her earlobe, sucked it into his mouth and flicked the delicate flesh with his tongue. She shivered against him, a moan gurgling in the back of her throat.

"Okay."

He laughed. "I love it when you're agreeable, Doc." Steve grabbed her hand and led her to the master bathroom.

6

GORDIE COULDN'T CATCH her breath, her ragged gasps for air echoing off the bathroom walls. Steve was on his knees, his mouth doing wicked things to her sex. The tricks he did with his tongue were going to kill her. She'd die a blissful death with a smile on her face. Her pussy clenched when he sucked her clit between his lips and licked. Shudders of delight danced across every nerve and splintered into blinding pleasure the second he thrust his fingers inside her.

Her hips bucked, rode the wave of her orgasm as the sensations went on and on. Gordie muffled a cry with her hand, bit into the soft flesh to stifle more. The sting of pain combined with the bliss of satisfaction made her legs shake. If it weren't for the wall behind her, she'd fall. Steve kept pushing and pumped his fingers faster, stroked her clit harder. He rimmed her anus and sent her into orbit as he pressed on the tight ring of muscle.

Newly initiated nerve endings spasmed and her lower belly drew tighter and tighter until she thought she'd snap. He slid his finger deeper into her ass and she broke like a twig under a size-eleven boot. No resistance. She shattered into a thousand pieces, her legs going out from under her. Steve removed his mouth and hand, catching her in his arms as she collapsed into his lap. Gordie's mind and body were limp and he wasted no time in maneuvering her to straddle his thighs.

He thrust up, drove his cock deep into her still-contracting channel. She wrapped her arms around his neck and leaned into him. Steve gripped her hips, held her suspended a few inches above him so he could raise and lower his pelvis, impaling her over and over on his erection. Muscles, lax from post-orgasmic euphoria sparked to life as he dragged his length over sensitive, swollen flesh. Blood coursed through her veins, hot and heavy, to drown her in renewed need.

"That's it. Come for me again." He tilted her hips, drove his body into hers at a different angle.

"I can't."

"Yes, you can," he panted as he continued to pound into her. "Once more, Doc."

"Oh God."

With a speed that was mind numbing, he took her up to the peak again. He showed no mercy, driving his cock in and out, hard and fast. Harsh breaths echoed around them, the tiled walls bounced the sound back to drum in her ears. Steve's mouth found hers, his tongue demanding she give all. She couldn't breathe, couldn't think, could only feel. Rapture so savage it slashed and destroyed her. Forgetting they weren't in the house alone, Gordie pulled her lips from his and screamed as another release tore through her.

Steve arched and sank balls-deep in her convulsing core. His hips jerked twice before he went rigid beneath her. He came, her name a hoarse groan that sounded more like a prayer for help than a cry of relief. She slumped against him, their torsos sticky with sweat. Their skin clung and their chests heaved with the desperate need for air. Her heart hammered double time against her ribs and her lungs burned but she couldn't move. Not yet.

"Wow." Steve lowered his back to the floor, taking her with him. "That was..."

"Yeah. It was." Her fingers and toes tingled as feeling started to return.

"We didn't even make it into the shower."

"Good thing we didn't. I need one more than ever now." She sighed.

"I don't know. I'm kinda partial to having my scent all over you."

Gordie lifted her head and found his gaze with hers. "I don't mind either. It's the copious amounts of sweat and sex smell I'm objecting to."

Steve buried his face into her neck and sniffed. "Smells pretty damn good to me. Good enough to eat." He nibbled at her throat.

A shiver traveled down her spine. "Stop it." The teasing bites tickled her skin and Gordie wiggled on top of him. His softened cock slipped from her body and warm sparks of arousal danced around in her lower belly. It amazed her to think she could have any interest left after their last encounter but each time they came together the need wasn't quenched. Instead it grew stronger, deeper.

He sucked on her neck, pulled her flesh between his lips with increasing pressure and Gordie knew she'd be left with a love bite when he was done. A ribbon of excitement snaked through her. The idea of others seeing Steve's mark thrilled her in a way she'd never imagined. She tipped her head sideways, gave him better access and moaned with her delight of being his.

"Damn you taste good," he murmured against her throat. "I could spend the entire day nibbling on you."

"Oh God. I could let you." Gordie pressed into him. Her body plastered to the length of his, their legs in a tangle.

"When?"

She squirmed as his mouth trailed wet kisses along her jaw. "What?"

"When can I nibble on you all day?" He licked the shell of her ear. "It can't be today but it has to be soon."

Gordie couldn't think. He was licking and biting and kissing every erogenous zone on her head. "Umm…"

"Christmas." More kisses. "Can I have you for Christmas dinner?" He stroked his tongue down to her shoulder, along her collarbone. "Spread out on my table with all the trimmings."

Oh God. He would kill her. "Please."

"Please what, Doc?" His teeth scraped over the slope of her breast.

"Anything," she gasped. "Everything."

He smiled against her skin. "Mmm, I can't wait for Christmas dinner."

Steve rolled her beneath him and sucked her nipple into his mouth. The cold floor at her back made her shiver. The heat of his body covering her front made her melt. He thrust his hips, his hard cock pressing into her thigh. She parted her legs, wrapped them around his waist and dug her heels into his ass to pull him closer. A growl vibrated over her breast a second before his teeth pinched the puckered tip and his cock entered her in one plunge.

"Ah, yes." Gordie's head tossed from side to side, the hard cold tile going unheeded as a blazing fire devoured her. He drove into her pussy and his erection rubbed over inflamed walls, sending her into sensory overload. Pleasure and pain. Pain and pleasure. Raw nerves no longer able to distinguish the difference, no longer cared, only needed to be taken. To give him everything he demanded.

~

STEVE BURIED his face against Doc's damp neck. He'd locked his elbows and braced his knees, but he struggled to keep his weight off her. His coyote was closer to breaking free than any other time they'd come together as satisfaction flowed through him. It amazed him that his wild side had been so quiet. The bizarre thing was he thought he understood why.

Doc had never run with any of the pack members that he knew of. Other than when Anthony had turned her and she'd run with the newly shifting teenagers of the pack, Steve couldn't recall her ever shifting. They'd change that over the next week. She needed to connect with that side of herself before his coyote could.

"When was the last time you shifted?" His lips brushed her skin and she shivered beneath him. "Shit. You're cold."

He rolled to the side and got to his feet. Reaching down he offered her his hand and pulled her from the floor. With her tucked into his side, he reached in and turned the shower on. In no time the water heated and steam billowed out to surround them. Gently, he nudged her in ahead of him.

"Come on, let's get clean and warm and then we can talk." He grabbed the soap and quickly lathered his hands.

Steve passed the bar to Doc and while she soaped up her hands he set to work washing her down. He didn't linger, couldn't afford to or his body would demand more of hers and neither of them needed that right now. If they weren't careful they'd wear each other out. A smile tipped his lips.

"What are you smiling at?" Her hands were busy cleaning his chest.

"Us. We're gonna kill each other with sex if we don't stop." Steve slid his hands over the curves of her hips.

"You started it."

"I didn't hear you complaining at all." He ran his hands up the inside of her thighs and she flinched. "Sore?"

"Tender. No, actually more sensitive, really, not sore."

Her delicate fingers trailed over his abs and he sucked in a breath, his cock pulsing with interest. "Jesus. We need to get some clothes on."

He stepped back out of temptation's touch and finished scrubbing himself down. Doc took the hint and did the same. Steve ignored the knowing smile on her lips and blanked out the wet, naked body in front of him. They really did need to head on back to his place where they'd have no interruptions and certainly no reason other than fatigue to keep their hands off each other.

Steve waited for Doc to step out and grab a towel. He couldn't stop his gaze from dropping to watch her sexy ass as she walked away from him. Mesmerized by the sight it took him a moment to realize she'd turned to offer him a towel and was in the process of covering up. With a sigh of disappointment he pulled it together and joined her on the bathmat.

"Why'd you ask about me shifting?" Doc had wrapped a second towel around her head and was vigorously rubbing the water from her hair.

"Because just now my coyote was closer to the surface than any other time we've had sex and it got me thinking about how quiet that side of me has been." Dry, he reached for his clothes.

"I don't shift very much."

"Why?"

She shrugged. "It's hard to explain, but after Anthony I kind of shut that side of myself down. And I guess because I was so newly turned I hadn't made that big of a connection with my coyote."

"Understandable. And now?"

"Around you or because we're together?"

"Both."

"Being around you always stirs me up, human and coyote, that's why I stayed away for so long. But after you moved away my coyote wouldn't let me stay too far. Hence the walks up in the forest near your place. Just being close to you calms her."

"So your coyote side is making its presence known." He slipped into his pants. "When we get home I'd like to shift together. I think we need to do that."

Gordie stumbled as she stepped into the borrowed sweats, she couldn't wait to be given the all clear to get into her room so she could grab some of her own clothes to wear. "Why?"

"Because it's part of who we are and I want to see you in coyote form. I've never seen you." Steve reached over and cupped her face in his hands. "And because I think you need to fully connect with your coyote side. I don't think you ever really have and the more we're together, the more our coyotes are going to want to bond."

She stared at him, her gaze searching his. He could feel her pulse beating against the heels of his hands. Steve waited, breath held, until she nodded. Releasing his breath in a slow stream, he bent forward and planted his mouth on hers. The kiss was nothing more than skin on skin, but he felt it to his bones and knew she did too. Her eyelids lowered and he took them deeper.

Her arms slid around his neck and her body pressed to his. Steve ran his tongue over the seam of her lips, pushed until she opened and let him inside. He explored the moist depths, licked and stroked and tasted every part of her. Breathless, he backed off, slowed his caresses and eased them out of the lush mating of their mouths.

Pulling back, he laid his forehead on hers and breathed deep. Her breathing came as harsh as his and her eyes remained closed. When her lids lifted to reveal her brown eyes he could see she'd fortified her emotions.

"No. No holding back, Doc. We agreed, no more arm's length. Talk to me." He moved back, gave her room to breathe.

"I'm scared."

"Why? What could possibly be frightening about shifting together?"

"I've never done it before."

"What? Shifted in front of another coyote?" That couldn't be right, surely she and Anthony had run together.

"I'm not good at it. It takes me ages to make the change. And I haven't run with anyone since Anthony turned me and I ran with the coming-of-age coyotes."

"You never shifted and ran with him?"

She bit her lip and shook her head.

"Ah, Doc." He tugged her close, nestled her face against his chest and wrapped his arms around her. "It's not hard and I don't care if it takes all day for you to shift into coyote form. Don't worry about it now. We'll deal with that side of us when we don't have any distractions."

He smoothed his hands up and down her spine, waited until he felt her tense muscles soften under his touch. A shuddery breath rattled her chest and her arms gave his waist one hard squeeze before she slipped from his embrace.

"I know I'm being irrational. I'm an educated woman, probably too educated, but I can't help the feelings inside me. I've felt like an outcast in this town my whole life. I always knew I was different even when I didn't understand why." She held up her hand to stop the protest he would have made. "I get that no one tried to make me feel that way, even those against half-bloods and non-bloods didn't single me out any more than anyone else, but that clawing desperation to be like everyone around me is what led me to accept a proposal I had no right to. I can't help thinking every decision I've made in these mountains has been a bad one."

"You never did anything wrong, Doc."

"I know that, really I do, but it'll play on my mind forever regardless of what I or anyone else thinks and I can't stop that from affecting the way I relate to my coyote. I hated that side of myself for years when I was away from here. It took me a long time to come to terms with who and what I am. Neither of us can expect me to come to terms with us and what that means quickly, Steve." She gripped his hand, curled her fingers between his. "I guess I'm asking you to be patient and in return I promise to try harder to connect to both you and myself."

Steve brushed a fingertip down her cheek. "Gordie, I think once you come to accept yourself there'll be no stopping us. And I think that will be the easy part of all of this."

"Hey." Dale banged on the bathroom door. "You two coming out anytime soon? Tatum's here with our lunch."

Doc smiled at him. "This seems to be turning into a habit."

"Yeah, it looks that way," he spoke softly. "We'll be out in a second," he called out to Dale.

"We'll be in the dining room. Kat sent over a feast and I'm starving so we're starting without you in five minutes," Tatum yelled.

Holding Doc's hand, Steve stepped over to the door and pulled her with him. "Come on or they'll eat all the good stuff before we get downstairs."

She laughed. "This is Kat's food, it's *all* good stuff."

Steve had to agree. Kat might grate on his nerves but she could cook better than anyone he'd ever known and that made up for every other flaw the woman had. Plus she was Doc's sister and he'd put up with anything and anyone to be with her.

They found Tatum and Dale already seated and loading their plates. He pulled out a chair for Doc and sat next to her as he grabbed the first bowl of food. It only took a few minutes to fill their plates and start eating. Nobody spoke until most of the food was polished off and their hunger abated.

Tatum pushed her chair back and laid a hand on her huge belly. "Damn that was good."

"You sure you've had enough?" Dale asked.

"Yep. I already ate a piece of chicken pie with potato and gravy while I waited for Kat to put the food together."

"You ate twice what I ate just now. Where the hell do you put it all? Other than that beach ball under your sweater there's nothing to you," Doc said.

Tatum grinned. "I know. I'm hoping that means I'll be back to my normal size once these two are born."

"Here. Drink some more tea." Dale refilled Tatum's cup. "You need fluids as well as food."

"Thanks."

Steve eyed his friend and wondered what he'd missed. Not twenty-four hours ago Dale and Tatum had been at each other's throats and now here they were getting on like the best of friends. He glanced at Doc but she only shrugged and kept on eating.

"I finished upstairs, Gordie. You can clean it up whenever you're ready," Dale said.

"Oh. Okay, thanks." She reached for her drink and took a sip. "Find anything?"

"No, nothing more than I expected to anyway. Both rooms had prints all over them but they could belong to anyone who's been in here over the last few months. I'll need to wait for the lab results before I can tell you anything else."

"I've bundled up the dresses. I'll take them out to Gramps' and see if Grammy can do anything about the stains. If anyone can fix them, it's Grammy," Tatum said.

"Thank you, Tatum. I'll let Rowan and El know." Doc leaned back in her chair with a sigh. "I'll have to ring Mom and tell her too."

"You don't have to ring her. Wait until she gets here," Steve offered.

"I guess it won't matter either way, will it? It's still going to hurt."

Steve placed his hand on her thigh. "Yeah, it will and I'm sure she'd rather hear it in person than over the phone."

"You're right. I'll wait until she gets here." Doc stood and began stacking plates. "Tatum, are you staying out at your grandparent's now that you've moved back home?"

"Um, no, I can't exactly expect Grammy and Gramps to put me and the babies up. Besides, I'll need to be closer to the clinic for work. I'm living in town."

Dale stood suddenly. "I'll give you a lift to the garage so you can pick up your car, Tatum."

"Oh. Okay. Do you mind if we leave you with the dishes, Doc? It's just that Harry said he'd be closing up right after lunch and I don't want to be without my car or my bags."

"Sure, go on. Steve will help clean up."

He swallowed the bite he'd just taken. "Do I have a choice?"

"Not really, but go ahead and finish eating. I'll wait." Doc grinned at him.

"Very polite of you," he grumbled.

"I know. My manners are impeccable." She left the plates on the table, patted him on the shoulder and walked toward the front of the house. "Don't worry about getting up, Steve, I'll see our guests out."

Steve could hear the laughter in her voice but had no intention of calling her on her cheek because she'd called them *our* guests. She probably didn't realize what she'd done. Without thought Gordie had tied them together in front of their friends. As far as he was concerned it was one huge step in the right direction.

GORDIE HELPED Tatum button up her coat and slip on her snow boots. "Did you want to start at the clinic after New Year? I know we said mid-to-late January but if you want to come in and get a feel for the place I'll be opening the doors again on the second."

"That would be great. I know a lot of the older generation but I'd like to meet everyone before I start taking over some of their care." Tatum took her handbag from Dale. "I've got your phone number so I'll ring you after Christmas and we can talk more about what it is you want and don't want."

"No need for that. We'll just get it all sorted when you start." She gave the other woman a hug. "Be sure to ring me if you have any concerns about your pregnancy. I worried about you changing doctors this far along but I'm thrilled that you feel safe enough to have these babies under my care."

"I'll be in touch if I get any lab results back but I doubt we'll hear anything before the New Year. There'll only be a skeleton staff on over the holidays." Dale opened the door and gestured for Tatum to precede him. "If anything else happens you know how to get hold of me."

"I do and thank you for everything you've done so far."

"It's my job, Gordie, but I'd be here even if it wasn't." He saluted and pulled the door closed as he stepped over the threshold.

"Alone at last."

Gordie jumped when Steve sneaked up behind her. "Jeez, don't do that."

"Sorry." He slid his arms around her waist. "We're not expecting any visitors for the rest of the day. It's a nice feeling having you all to myself."

She leaned back. "Yeah, but we'll be too busy cleaning to notice." Gordie sighed. "I don't know where to start."

"Kitchen. We'll tidy up the lunch dishes, check out what Kat sent over for dinner and breakfast before we tackle upstairs." Steve spun her to face him. "It won't take the two of us long and then we can start packing up some of your things."

"Are we still staying here tonight?"

"Did you not look outside when the others left? It's snowing again. The storm is supposed to be short lived but I doubt we'll be finished before dark so I thought we'd stick around here, have breakfast in the morning and then head over to The Den for lunch and then on home after that. Sound good?"

"Kat's expecting us to be at the dinner table on Christmas day."

"Not going to happen. The storm they're predicting for Christmas morning will keep everyone inside for a couple of days. That's why I thought we could appease her with lunch tomorrow."

"Okay." She sucked in a deep breath. "I guess we should get this over with."

Steve let her go. "Lead the way."

It didn't take them long in the kitchen and all too soon she had to deal with the mess upstairs. They started in Kat's room and Gordie cried the whole time she put piece after piece of her sister's doll collection into the garbage bags they were using. The wall would need repainting after she'd used a good paint stripper on it, although it might be worth ripping the drywall down and having new boards fitted.

She took a bag out of the room and went to get the vacuum. There were thousands of shards from the shattered porcelain embedded in the carpet. Gordie wasn't sure, but she wouldn't be surprised if the carpet would need to be replaced. Steve took the cord and plugged it in before shooing her out of the room.

"I'll do this. You go get clean sheets so you can make the bed when I'm done."

They'd stripped what was left of the bedding, the quilt had been an old one and rather than attempt to remove the slivers of ceramic she'd chosen to throw it out. She'd have to do the same with the one in her room. The thought made her cry all over again. Her Grandmother Monroe had made the quilt for her when she'd first come to live in Whispering Springs. Gordie had only gotten four years with her before she'd died, but Granny Roe had been the only grandparent she'd ever had.

Gordie pulled linen from the cupboard, the smell of her mother's favorite scent billowing out to surround her. It was a comfort, made her feel as though her mother was there with her, giving her a hug. Arms loaded up, she went back to Kat's old room and leaned against the doorjamb. Steve worked the vacuum as if he did it every day. Watching him do something so domestic gave her heart a jolt. He kept surprising her with his strength and his willingness to stand beside her no matter what.

The man plowed roads, built houses, did dishes and vacuumed floors. Her only experience living with a man other than her stepfather was Anthony and he'd been one of those men who firmly believed in women's work and men's work and never the twain shall meet. Steve was turning all she'd known and expected on its head but she wasn't upset. In fact she was thrilled to discover he thought of them as equals, both of them pitching in no matter what needed to be done.

"What are you smiling at?"

She hadn't realized he'd stopped the machine. Pushing off the wall, Gordie walked over and threw an arm around his neck. His height meant she had to stand on her toes but she planted her mouth on his for a quick kiss.

"Thank you," she said as she settled back on her feet.

"You're welcome but I'm not sure what I'm being thanked for." He smiled down at her.

"For being here. For standing beside me. For being you."

"All that huh?" His smile turned into a grin. "I guess you should be pretty thankful. Although, that kiss doesn't seem like enough payment for me being such a stand-up guy."

"Oh no you don't. You've had plenty of payment in the last twenty-four hours."

"I thought that was an even split of income. Seemed to me as though you were getting paid just as much."

Gordie's stomach fluttered and her pussy clenched, moisture dampened her panties. "We need to clean the house."

"We've been cleaning. I think we need to both get paid before we clean any more." He picked her up and stepped over the vacuum.

"Steve." Even to her own ears the protest held no strength.

"Gordie."

"We shouldn't."

Steve grinned down at her. "Yeah we should."

He lowered his head and kissed her. His tongue tangled with hers as they each sought to claim the other. They bumped their way into her parents' room and Steve put her down and started removing their clothes. Her shirt went, then his. He pulled the drawstring on her pants and pushed them down. She tugged his sweats over his hips. Each of them toed off their shoes and by the time they hit the mattress only their socks remained.

They hadn't bothered to pull the bedding back but neither of them noticed the wedding ring quilt beneath them. Engrossed in touching and tasting, they both took and gave with equal measure. Steve drove her to the peak quickly. Her orgasm broke over her in a tumble of sensation and need. But he wasn't done. With care he pushed her back up. This time slow and sensual led the way to the top. And when he finally came inside her they took the last steps together. He continued to thrust inside her until her release ebbed away. Spent but satisfied, she curled into his side and drifted off to sleep.

STEVE LET Doc sleep while he cleaned the rest of Kat's room. Too restless to sleep, he knew he'd be tempted to wake her up and have her again if he stayed in bed. Besides, he didn't want to be in the room when she worked out they'd broken the *not in my parents' bed* rule. The thought of how they'd smashed her rule made him smile as he hauled the last bag of garbage down the stairs.

The snow had stopped a few minutes ago but already the temperature was dropping inside the house. He walked around looking for the thermostat controls to check it was switched on. It wasn't until he'd walked the entire downstairs that he found the control box on the wall inside the little mudroom off the kitchen. Someone had the temp set too low so he turned the dial and waited for the furnace to kick in.

He waited several minutes but nothing happened and he was about to head down into the basement to check the heating system when Doc came into the kitchen.

"You finished off Kat's room."

"There wasn't much left to do and unlike you, I was awake."

"You should have woken me." She walked over to him. "What's wrong?"

"I was going to check the furnace. I turned up the heat but I haven't heard the unit start up yet." Steve pulled the door to the basement open.

"Hang on, the globe down there blew the other day, I'll grab a flashlight." She stepped into the mudroom and returned with a large flashlight.

"That looks more like a weapon than a light."

She grinned. "It's a two-for-one deal."

"A what?"

"Two-for-one. Two tools in one piece of equipment." Doc lifted the black stick above her head. "Anyone bothers me I can smash them over the head with it. Or I can switch it on and blind them before they get close enough to be any trouble."

"Wow." He ducked his head. "Remind me not to sneak up on you in a dark alley."

"I'm not about to find myself in a dark alley and I'd be concerned if I found you in one." She switched on the light and aimed it on the stairs. "I'll lead the way, I know where I'm going and I'd hate for you to fall down the stairs or trip over one of the million boxes Mom has stored down here."

They reached the furnace to find the pilot light had gone out. He was familiar with the unit so it only took a few minutes to ignite and have heat pumping through the venting pipes. As they turned to go back upstairs the flashlight hit on something to their right that made him reach out and grab Doc's hand to redirect the beam back to what he'd glimpsed.

Doc gasped and her hand trembled under his, the spotlight dancing over the plastic dry-cleaners bags. Steve plucked the flashlight from her grasp and quickly scanned the room. Nothing else looked out of place and other than the bags everything had a layer of dust to show how long they'd been down here. He entwined his fingers with Doc's and led the way back to the kitchen.

Once out of the dark he switched off the flashlight and placed it on the kitchen table on his way to the back door. He checked for signs of forced entry knowing full well that Dale had done that earlier but Steve had to see for himself. Next he checked windows, from one room to the next until he found himself at the front door. Doc followed behind, her hand still in his.

"What are we doing?" she asked.

"Checking for how the fucking bastard got inside."

"But Dale checked already."

"I know." He turned to look at her. "I need to see for myself."

"Okay."

They made their way upstairs and one by one he checked all the windows. There were no balconies so no outside doors and Steve was just about to concede defeat when he happened to glance up the hallway. At the far end from where they stood was a manhole in the ceiling and the square removable section appeared crooked.

"What type of roofing do you have?" he asked as he headed for the other end of the house.

"Type? Oh, you mean shingles or tin sheeting? Shingles, why?" She was right on his heels.

He stared up at the recently moved manhole and said, "Because I think I just worked out how he got into your house."

Steve pulled his phone out of his pocket and dialed the sheriff.

"Dale Turner."

"I know how he got in."

"How? I searched that house from top to bottom."

"I know. Also, we found dry-cleaning bags in the basement."

"Shit. Didn't the deputies look down there?"

"Yeah, but to be honest I doubt they would have realized what they were. I only recognized them because I picked up my suit last week and I knew where the dresses had gone missing from."

"Right. I'm still going to ream them a new one. Now tell me how you think Marcus is getting in that house."

"Through the roof."

"The roof?"

"Yep. I'm staring at the manhole in the upstairs hall. It's been moved recently and it hasn't been put back in the grooves properly so it's sitting lopsided."

"Give me five minutes to finish up here and I'll be over."

"Okay. See you in a few." Steve hung up and put the phone in his pocket.

"Do you really think he got in that way?" Doc asked.

He turned to look at her. "Yeah, it looks that way to me."

"So Dale's coming back?"

"Yep." He gripped her elbow and steered her toward the stairs. "Why don't we put a pot of coffee on and wait for him in the kitchen?"

"I'll make a pot but I'm boiling the kettle for some tea. I've had enough coffee for today."

Steve let Doc fuss over the tea and coffee making but it didn't escape his notice that her hands trembled. Maybe they shouldn't stay here tonight. She might feel safer back at his place or they could crash at Kat's.

"We're staying here." Her voice held a trace of anger. "I know what you're thinking and we're not letting him drive us out of here."

He glanced at the clock on the oven. "Well, it's too late to head up the mountain to my place and I guess Kat doesn't have room in that apartment of hers."

"No, she doesn't. We're staying put."

"Okay." Steve stood when the knock came on the front door. "I'll get it."

Steve opened the door and let Dale in. "Thanks for coming so quickly. Again."

"Anytime. Now where's the manhole?"

"Upstairs, end of the hall in front of the senior Monroe's bedroom."

"Okay, I'll go up and take a look. I'll give you a yell if I want to get up in the roof."

"Doc's making coffee so come on down for a cup when you've had a look and then we'll get up in the roof together. I'm not leaving it. I want to take a look up there to make sure none of the shingles have been moved."

"Will do." Dale turned and headed up the stairs two at a time.

Steve went back to the kitchen. Doc had poured a tea and sat at the table with a slice of what looked like chocolate cake.

"Is that what I think it is?" He pointed to her plate.

"If you think its Kat's special recipe, double-choc chocolate cake, then yes it is." She grinned and forked a piece of cake into her mouth. "Mmm..."

"Where is it?" He opened the fridge and peered inside. "I can't see it."

"Here."

Steve turned to find her placing a second plate with a slice of cake on the table. "That's not a very big bit," he complained.

"I know, but she only sent a small section of the cake, not the whole thing. I'm saving some for dessert."

He took the chair in front of the cake. "Quick, let's eat it before Dale gets down and wants some. I'm not sharing this with him if we don't have a whole cake."

"Don't worry, Kat packed some chocolate chip cookies so Dale can have those with his coffee."

"What?" Steve's fork paused halfway to his mouth. "Cookies? Damn, I'm gonna get fat at this rate."

Doc laughed. "Probably. I can't cook so I usually pick up dinner at the café before I head home every night."

Steve groaned. "Oh yeah, I'm gonna get fatter than Santa."

"Well as long as you have his cheery disposition we'll get along just fine."

"Having you sit on my lap and tell me your most secret desire is guaranteed to keep me in a cheery mood."

"Is that coffee I smell?" Dale asked as he entered the room. "No, don't get up, I'll pour my own."

Steve scraped up the last piece of cake and shoved it in his mouth. "There's cookies too."

Doc stood and went to the counter. "Here, let me get that for you, Dale."

"I'm fine, Gordie, sit back down so we can talk."

"You think I'm right?" Steve asked.

"Yeah." Dale brought his mug and plate to the table. "It looks like he came in through the roof to me too."

"Are you sure?" Doc asked.

"No, but we will be after we've had our coffee and gone up to look inside that manhole." Dale took a bite of cookie and closed his eyes.

"You're going up there?"

"Yes. We need to make sure all the shingles are in place or you'll get snow and water in the cavity and be in all sorts of trouble," Steve said.

"There's a step ladder in the mudroom. You can use that to reach the ceiling." Doc got up and disappeared into the small outer room. She came back carrying a five-rung, steel ladder. "The flashlight is on the counter. If you two don't mind I think I'll get started on cleaning my room."

"I'll be up in a second," Steve called after her. "Is it possible he got into the clinic the same way?" he asked Dale when he was sure she was out of earshot.

"Definitely. We'll take a look at that tomorrow, it's too late now."

"Okay. I'll take the ladder up. Finish your coffee and cookies, there's no rush unless you've got somewhere to be."

Dale looked startled for a moment but quickly masked the look with his usual, bland sheriff face. "Nope. Nowhere to be."

7

GORDIE SAT beside Tatum at the counter of The Den Café. Steve had dropped her here an hour ago to hang out with Kat before they headed up to his place for the rest of the week. Tatum had already been here and Doc's sister was busy bustling back and forth from the kitchen making all the meals that people would be picking up for the Christmas feast tomorrow. She'd explained to Kat about not spending the meal together and surprisingly Kat hadn't argued.

They'd spent the morning at the clinic with the sheriff. He'd insisted she walk through each of the rooms looking for anything that Marcus may have left behind. Unfortunately there was nothing new to discover and it seemed pointless to fingerprint when there must be hundreds of different prints throughout the building, but Dale did anyway. There was nothing in the roof space to suggest Marcus had been there either. After they'd finished Steve had wanted to go back to her parents house and check the roof in daylight to be sure there were no broken shingles or clues that may lead to Marcus' whereabouts. Rather than go with him she'd opted to stay here.

Kat came through the swinging timber half-doors from the kitchen and placed two steaming bowls of soup in front of Gordie and Tatum. She walked down the counter and pulled two fresh bread rolls from a basket and brought them back to them.

"Eat. It'll warm you up and fill your bellies." Kat eyed Tatum's nonexistent waist. "Not that your belly needs any more filling."

Tatum laughed. "You're right, but I expect to be filled out more before this pregnancy is over."

"How are you feeling? No cramping or sickness?" Gordie asked as she spooned up a mouthful of soup.

"No. Although, if you don't mind, can I pick up a blood pressure kit from the clinic before you leave town? My feet are a little swollen, but I think that's normal. And the usual backache but again, that's the same as it's been the whole pregnancy." Tatum dipped her roll into the bowl and took a bit. "Mmm..." She spoke around the mouthful. "This is delicious. Can I get some to take home with me?"

"Sure, I'll make you up a Christmas feast pack for three." Kat grinned and headed back to the kitchen again.

"God, your sister can cook."

"I know. She got all the domestic skills in the family."

"You can't cook?"

"I won't poison anyone but I can't make heaven the way Kat can."

"Damn. That sucks."

"Not really. I just stop by here every night I'm in the mood for something delicious."

"I think I'm going to be doing that. I can cook, not as well as this but I do all right. It's just lately I can't find the energy to walk, never mind stand around and cook. I fall asleep at the drop of a hat."

"That's to be expected, you are carrying twins."

"Yes, but I can't believe how easily I tire. Take the other night at Steve's. I'd walked from my car and by the time I reached the driveway I was exhausted. I could have literally slid to the ground asleep if I'd let myself. As it was, I knew I couldn't go any farther. Lucky Dale and Steve found me when they did. That never would have happened before I got pregnant." Tatum rubbed her belly. "I'm starting to get tired now so I'll need to head home soon. I'll finish this yummy soup first though, not passing this up for sleep, that's for sure."

"We'll walk over and grab that kit before you go."

"Thanks."

They finished their soup without another word spoken. Gordie let Kat know where they were going and what they were doing.

"Don't you want to wait for Steve to come back?" her sister asked.

"I don't know how much longer he'll be and Tatum needs to get home soon so she can rest. It's just across the road, Kat, and Steve and Dale went over the place this morning so I know there's no one lurking around. Besides, we'll only be a couple of minutes at the most."

"Okay, but if you're not back in ten minutes I'm coming after you." Kat came around the counter to walk them to the door.

Gordie helped Tatum into her coat before pulling on her own. Kat handed them their gloves and hats.

"Watch the sidewalk. It's bound to be icy."

Taking each step with care, Gordie held onto Tatum's arm as they traversed the slippery footpath. There was no traffic on the road so they crossed over at a leisurely stroll to be sure they didn't trip. Gordie led them around the rear of the building.

"We have to go in the back way. The front door has two

slide bolts on the inside that you can't open from the street." Gordie pulled her keys from her pocket as they walked up the back lane. "Careful, there are a couple of potholes beneath the snow near that fence."

"I'm watching. Believe me, after the first few times of finding myself flat on my ass I take every step with care. I was never clumsy before I got pregnant."

"I won't ask because it's none of my business but you have to know everyone in town is going to be curious about the father. You ought to think about what you're going to tell everyone before the questions start."

"By the time I see the rest of the pack I'll have an answer ready. For now though I'd rather stay quiet on the subject."

"Okay." They reached the back door and Gordie slid the key into the padlock and then the two deadlocks. "Let's get in out of the cold."

The clinic was dark and freezing, no warmer than outside but at least they were out of the wind. Gordie flicked the light switch and the gloom vanished. She pushed the door closed behind them and led Tatum through the building, giving her a brief rundown of what each room was used for.

"I'll give you the full tour on your first day but for now let me grab that kit." Gordie started back to the storeroom.

"Mind if I just sit here for a minute? I'm suddenly tired enough for my legs to shake," Tatum said.

"No, that's fine. If it's okay with you I might just give you a quick once-over before we head back to the café."

"Sure." Tatum covered a yawn with her hand. She smiled. "Sorry, really tired."

"Why don't you come into the exam room and lie down for a bit?"

"No way. I do that and I won't get up until I've had at least an hour's nap."

"I've got nowhere to be in a hurry."

"Thanks, but no. I want to get home and curl up in a nice, warm bed."

"Okay. I'll be back in a second."

Gordie left Tatum to rest while she went to the supply room. She was occupied scanning the shelves for the new kit she'd recently ordered in preparation for her nurse starting work when the hair on the back of her neck stood on end as though a cold wind had blown across her skin. She'd shut the back door hadn't she? Locked it? Footsteps echoed behind her and her stomach clenched. Leaning out the door of the storeroom she glimpsed a flash of black disappearing into the reception area where she'd left Tatum.

A shiver rattled her spine and her heart sped up. Gordie stepped into the hall as Tatum's cry of distress reverberated off the walls. Her feet moved before the thought formed and she ran the length of the corridor.

"No!"

Gordie could hear Tatum's struggles before she entered the waiting room. She skidded to a halt at the sight of a familiar-looking man in black. Every hackle rose and sweat popped out of every pore as she remained frozen in place while the two figures fought.

"Gordie, run!" Tatum's shout got Gordie moving again.

Her heart pounded against her ribs and her lungs refused to take more than small gulps of air. She would not let him win this time. There wasn't much in the way of weapons in the clinic but she could improvise. Gordie picked up the bundle of magazines on the corner table and threw them at the mass of wrestling bodies. It was enough to draw the masked attacker's attention away from Tatum.

With a growl he shoved Tatum aside and came at Gordie. Spinning on her heel she ran toward the room most likely to hold some kind of weapon. The morgue. Moments ago the hallway had seemed short, now it appeared to go on forever before she reached her destination. Trays of sterile surgical implements sat to one side of the large room and Gordie headed straight for them. Scooping up a handful of plastic-covered steel, she darted around the end of an exam table, putting the slab of cold metal between her and Marcus.

She had no doubt who hid behind the ski mask. Gordie would never forget those eyes. He'd been wearing the same clothes two days ago so it was obvious who had returned. Tatum hadn't made a sound after he'd flung her against the wall and the doctor in Gordie wanted to go check to see if the other woman was all right but she couldn't afford to let her guard down or neither of them would be okay.

"You can't hide from me, non-blood bitch." His shout echoed down the hall.

Gordie crouched down behind the table and peered around the pedestal base to watch the doorway. If he kept going she could sneak out of the room and back to Tatum. His heavy foot-falls grew closer.

"I'll kill you when I get my hands on you." He was moving from room to room, searching for her.

Fear sliced into her. He outweighed her by at least one hundred pounds, probably more, but Gordie knew the soft spots, knew where to strike to inflict the most damage if she had to.

"You can't hide and that bitch out front isn't going to save your sorry ass from what I've got planned."

His words chilled her blood, the venom in them unmistak-able. She also couldn't miss the slight tinge of madness ringing in his voice. Gordie knew he'd checked most of the other rooms, knew it was only a matter of time before he reached this one and she needed a plan. Two plans. One for when he found her and one for if he passed on by.

"You're going to pay for all the trouble you've caused."

Trouble? What trouble? Gordie had no idea what he was talking about. She'd never had much to do with Marcus. He'd always considered her beneath him because she was human and then after Anthony had died he'd never even glanced her way. He hadn't even come to her for medical treatment once since she'd taken over the clinic from her stepfather.

"You think you're so smart hooking up with that McKenna bastard." He was in the next room, moving closer with every breath.

She fingered the plastic packets in her hands, glanced down quickly to see exactly what she had. Three scalpels, two sets of forceps and two pairs of scissors. What would she do with the forceps? A sound in the doorway drew her gaze. Black boots and jeans up to the knee were visible. She wasn't game to move for a better look. Gordie watched those boots intently. The second he came toward her or left she'd be ready.

He turned and went back into the hall. Air rushed from her chest, hissed through her teeth as relief filled her. Gordie carefully removed the plastic from the instruments and counted to one hundred before standing and tiptoeing toward the door. She couldn't hear anything and that worried her more than having him in the doorway in front of her would have. Soundlessly, she made her way across the room.

Her skin prickled and instinct made her jump back seconds before he charged into the room. He reached for her throat, his hands wrapping around her neck and hooking in her jacket as she tried to spin away. The zipper on her coat dug into her skin and she gagged as her airway was crushed. Gordie brought her hand up, scissors extended and drove them into the nearest body part. Cloth tore and skin broke as she pushed with all her strength. Marcus howled in pain and his grip loosened, allowing her to twist free of his hold.

"Bitch!" He'd removed his mask, his gaunt face skeletal in appearance and a mere impression of his former self.

Marcus lunged for her, the scissors protruding from between the fourth and fifth ribs near the center of his chest. His fingers caught her sleeve and he wrenched her back against him. The steal handles of the scissors dug into her shoulder and she applied pressure to drive them deeper. A curse filled her ears and he shoved her forward, sent her tumbling to the floor. Pain exploded in her back as she went down and she rolled away just before he kicked out a second time.

"Not so fucking tough now are you?" He lashed out with his foot again, grazing her hip with the toes.

Gordie grabbed at his pants, tangled her fingers in the fabric and pulled. He teetered above her so she gave the jeans another yank and sent him crashing to the ground beside her. She clambered for purchase but she slid on the slippery tile beneath her hands and feet. Steal glinted next to her and she realized she'd dropped her makeshift weapons in their struggle. Reaching out, she wrapped her fingers around the nearest one.

"Fucking bitch!" Marcus crawled after her.

With desperation she lashed out, but he dodged to the side and the blade of a scalpel glanced along his cheek, barely leaving a scratch. He kept coming, managed to pin her beneath him, his body crushing hers. She kicked and punched, bucked and thrashed in an attempt to dislodge him. Marcus tangled his fingers in her hair and used his grip to slam her head into the ground repeatedly. Stars burst before her eyes and Gordie's arms flailed about without purpose.

He was going to kill her. There was no way she could throw

him off, he was too heavy. Tears burned her eyes and throat as he once again wrapped his hands around her neck and began to squeeze. The back of her head pounded but the pain had begun to go numb. Her arms and legs wouldn't work properly, their weight too much to move. Her vision blurred, blackness creeping in around the edges and she thought she heard someone call her name.

Steve.

"He's too late." Marcus laughed above her, his face a grotesque, distorted image. "You're dead, bitch, and he's next."

"No." The hoarse cry hurt her throat but she couldn't let him get Steve. With the last of her energy Gordie lifted her arm, the scalpel still in her hand, and slashed out at his face. At first she thought she'd missed. Marcus stopped squeezing and his mouth fell open. Everything happened in slow motion. For seconds neither of them breathed and then blood began to bead in a long line down the side of his neck. The beading quickly turned to a flow.

The flow increased rapidly until blood pumped from the slice in gushing waves. She'd hit his carotid artery. Marcus let go of her throat and grabbed his neck but he couldn't stop the surge. He fell to the side and Gordie used her hands and feet to scramble backward. She slipped and slid in the pool of blood forming on the floor, the slick warmth made her move quicker in a bid to get away. But it was all around her, over her. His hands fell from his body as he collapsed with the gurgle of his final breath in his throat.

Gordie stared at Marcus' lifeless body, the sea of red spreading out around him and began to tremble. Tears streamed down her cheeks as she curled into a ball and brought her hands up to cover her face. Sobs racked her chest, the heaving gasps compressing her ribs and stomach with pain.

Wetness soaked into her clothes and she uncovered her eyes to see nothing but the blood she'd spilled surrounding her.

A cry of anguish echoed in the room, the sound vibrating in her ears as her scream of agony went on and on.

STEVE WALKED into the café with Dale. They'd spent the morning combing the clinic and then the roof cavity at Doc's place but other than a few broken shingles they hadn't found any more clues. He headed for the counter, searching the room for Doc as he went, but he couldn't see her anywhere. Kat was serving a customer so he slid onto a stool and waited for her to finish.

"Do you want to check the roof at the clinic again before you head home?" Dale asked.

"No. We'll do that before she opens up again though. I want it checked before she goes back there."

Kat put a couple of mugs down and filled them with coffee. "Can I get you something to eat?"

"No thanks, coffee's fine. Where's Doc?" he asked.

"She and Tatum walked over to the clinic to get something for Tatum."

Steve jumped from his seat. "Alone? You let them go alone?" He headed for the door at a run, dodging tables and chairs on the way.

"What's wrong? She said you'd checked it this morning. That it was safe," Kat protested behind him.

"We did," he yelled as he yanked the door open. "But I don't want her going there alone."

Dale was right behind him when he hit the sidewalk. They ran across the empty street and skidded to a stop at the front door. Steve tried the handle and finding it locked, began thumping on the door and calling out to Doc.

"Wait." Dale grabbed Steve's arm. "Listen."

He turned his head and held his breath. The murmured cry for help was barely audible through the thick timber panel. "That doesn't sound like Doc."

Dale put his ear to the door but he didn't need to, the next cry came through loud and clear. "What the fuck? Tatum!" Dale banged on the door.

Steve started down the sidewalk at a flat-out run as his stomach cramped with the fear that threatened to take him to his knees. *Where the hell was Gordie?*

"Where are you going?" Dale yelled behind him.

"Around the back." He breathed hard but kept running, Dale's footsteps pounding behind him. "We'll never break down the front door but there's a window above the back one."

Steve would smash through the timber wall if he had to. He ran past the clothing store, the small bookshop and slid sideways in the snow as he rounded the corner of the building. The alley was unplowed and he could see footprints where Doc and Tatum had walked. As he got closer to the back of the clinic he was hit by déjà vu. The back door stood ajar and his blood ran cold.

"Let me go in first." Dale had caught up to him and pulled his gun from its holster.

"Fine, but I'm right behind you."

They entered the building at a slower pace. Dale took the lead but Steve stayed right on his heels. No sounds came from the interior and he thought maybe they'd imagined the cry from Tatum. The sight that met them in the morgue almost crippled him. Doc lay curled on her side, covered in blood. A huge pool of the stuff lay between her and Marcus. Neither of them appeared to be breathing.

Steve dropped to the floor next to Doc and felt for a pulse. The hard, fast beat he found in her neck produced a gust of breath from his lungs. He tried to find her injuries but the blood was everywhere, he couldn't tell where any of it was coming from. "I can't find where she's bleeding."

Dale checked Marcus. "I'm not sure it's her blood. He's dead, looks like she slashed his throat."

"Jesus. What the fuck happened?" He tapped Doc's cheek. "Doc? Come on, Gordie, talk to me."

"I'll be back. I need to find Tatum." Dale left the room with his gun drawn.

"Come on, Gordie, don't do this to me. Not again." He turned to the doorway as people started pouring into the room. "Stay back," he yelled.

"Dad's here," Kat said as Doctor Monroe pushed past the cluster of bodies.

"Hey, Steve." The older man kneeled beside him. "What you got?"

"Don't know. She was out when we found her."

Doctor Monroe ignored the lifeless body not six feet away and went to work on his daughter. "Jackie, get over here and help me with our girl."

"I'll do it. What do you want?" Steve asked.

"Let's get her checked over for broken bones first then we'll get her up on one of those tables."

"Can we move her into another room?" Jackie asked as she crouched beside them.

"Yes, love, that might be a better idea." Doctor Monroe turned to yell over his shoulder. "Kat, go get one of the rooms ready."

"Okay, Dad."

"And the rest of you can get out," the older man said with an authoritative voice Steve remembered from his youth.

"Doctor Monroe?" Dale came in carrying an semi-conscious Tatum.

"Jesus, Mary and Joseph. What went on here?" He turned to his wife, his hands never leaving Gordie. "Jackie, go with Dale and see about that one for me. I'll bring Gordana in a minute."

The older man spent what felt like hours checking Doc over before speaking again.

"Young man, I'm gonna ask you to carry Gordie for me. These old bones aren't as strong as they used to be."

"Yes sir."

Steve waited for Doc's father to get up before pulling her limp body into his arms. He stepped across the wet floor with care and ignored the way his boots stuck to the tiles as he walked down the hall behind Doctor Monroe. They passed the first room where Dale and Jackie were talking to a now-awake Tatum and entered the next one. Kat waited for them, closing the door behind him as he cleared the threshold.

"Get her out of those clothes so I can clean her up," Doctor Monroe ordered as he went to the sink in the corner and scrubbed his hands.

Steve laid Doc on the table and helped Kat remove her bloody clothes. They threw them in the trash. Even if they were salvageable he was sure she wouldn't want them. He was relieved to find no visible wounds other than some bruising and the angry red ringing her neck. The thought of what those red marks meant boiled his blood and if Marcus wasn't already lying dead in the other room Steve would be out committing murder right now.

"Steve?" Doc's voice was a raw, gravelly whisper that hurt his ears, he could only imagine how it felt to her.

He finished tucking the blanket around her and leaned closer. "I'm here, Doc."

"Tatum?"

"She's in the next room. Your mother is looking after her."

"Mom's here?"

"Me too, sweet girl." Doctor Monroe stepped up beside the bed.

"Daddy?"

"Hey, sweetie, wanna tell me what hurts?"

"Everything." A slight smile curled her lips. "Nothing's broken. Took a kick in the back and hip, he bashed my head into the floor and tried to choke me." Her hand came up and brushed against her throat.

"I see that. You don't look so bad, considering." Doctor Monroe took the wet cloth Kat handed him. "We're just gonna clean you up a bit, you can take a shower back at the house later."

"What happened to Marcus?" she asked.

"He's dead." Doctor Monroe wiped the cloth over her face, removing the dried blood.

The color drained from Doc's face. "Dead?" She licked her lips. "I'm gonna be sick."

Steve grabbed the waste basket and shoved it under her as she leaned over the side of the bed and emptied out her stomach. Her father held her hair back and Kat handed Steve a clean cloth when Doc had finished vomiting.

"I want to go home." She slumped back against the pillow.

"Okay, I'll get your mother to take you while I check on our other patient."

"No."

"No?"

"I don't want to go back to the house." She turned away and curled into a ball.

Steve took pity on the older man. "Can I talk to you outside, sir? Kat, keep an eye on Doc."

They stepped into the hall as Mrs. Monroe came out of the other room, Dale and Tatum behind her.

"Hey, you okay?" Steve asked.

"Yeah, a little embarrassed at passing out and not helping Doc, but otherwise I'm good." Tatum leaned into Dale.

"I'll talk to you later, Steve. I'm taking Tatum home to rest. Brogan and Quinn arrived a little while ago. They're handling the Marcus issue with the help of my deputies."

"Need me to do anything?"

"No. Just take care of Doc."

Steve watched as Dale and Tatum headed for the back door.

"Want to tell us what's going on, son?" Doctor Monroe asked.

"I'll keep it short for now but the bare bones are this. Marcus has led a terror campaign against Doc, Gordie, for a few months. As usual, she's weathered it all on her own, but two days ago he stepped it up and the results are..." Steve tried to think of the best words to describe his and Doc's new relationship.

"You and my daughter are mated." Mrs. Monroe saved him the trouble.

He felt his cheeks heat. "Yes."

Doctor Monroe slapped him on the back. "About time you pulled your head out of your ass, boy."

"With all due respect, dear, I think it's Gordana who's had her head up her ass," Mrs. Monroe said.

Steve smiled. He'd forgotten how much he liked the Monroes. Being the town's only doctor and nurse, they'd been a huge part of his growing-up years. And now they'd be his in-laws.

"If it's okay with the two of you, I'd like to take Doc home with me tonight. I know we'll probably be stuck up the mountain for a few days with the storm due in tomorrow but I think she's going to need the time to recuperate."

"Son, I think her physical recovery will be far easier than the mental one. She took a life today. That won't sit well with her no matter how deserving the bastard was." Doctor Monroe held out his hand. "And I guess I should say welcome to the family."

Steve shook the other man's hand. "Thank you, sir."

"None of that *sir* business now, we're family after all." He turned to Mrs. Monroe. "Let's go get that girl of ours ready to go home."

He gave them a few minutes with their daughter. They hadn't seen each other in months and coming home to this couldn't be easy to deal with. The commotion at the other end of the hall drew his attention and he wandered down to see what was going on. Brogan and Quinn were making sure the deputies did their job, but Steve didn't think it really mattered. Marcus was dead and couldn't be punished for any of his crimes.

"Hey. How's Doc?" Brogan asked when he saw Steve standing in the doorway.

"Okay as she can be. She came out with minor physical damage, but I'm not sure about the emotional yet." Steve ran a hand over his head, dragged his fingers through his hair.

"You heading home?" Quinn asked.

"Yeah, Doctor and Mrs. Monroe are with her now. I'll let them have a few minutes and then we'll head out."

"Gordie's going with you? She isn't going home with the Monroes?" Brogan asked.

"She doesn't want to go home with them. Doctor Monroe seems to understand it better than I do though. I thought for sure she'd want to be with them."

"She needs her mate," Quinn said.

"I guess, but she's fought against it for so long I can't see that it would be this easy."

"It's not going to be easy, Steve." Kat came up beside him. "She's shutting down. She won't talk to any of us. Mom and Dad are just getting her dressed, where's your truck?"

"Shit. Down the street. I'll go get it, bring it around the back."

"Okay. I'll let Gordie know that's what you're doing." Kat walked back down the hall.

"I'll talk to you guys later." Steve waved as he headed out the back door.

GORDIE ALLOWED her mother and father to fuss over her. It must have been a shock for them to arrive home and find the mess she'd found herself in. They'd avoided the subject and while she was glad, she knew it meant rehashing the event later but right now she just wanted to forget everything that had happened in the last few days. The door opened and Steve came in. Well, maybe not everything.

"Ready to go home?" he asked.

Home. Such a simple word. One she thought she understood the meaning of until she'd taken that final step with Steve. Home wasn't a house to her anymore. Home was Steve.

"Yes. Take me home." She held her arms out and he stepped into her, lifting her off her feet for a full-body hug. Gordie buried her face in the warmth of his neck and bit her lip to stifle the tears threatening to fall. She refused to fall apart yet.

"We'll see you all in a few days," Steve said as he carried her from the room.

Gordie didn't look up or say goodbye to her parents or sister and she certainly didn't raise her head as Steve walked through the clinic. She didn't want to chance seeing anything again today. There'd be plenty of time in the coming weeks to deal with the clinic and the carnage Marcus had caused.

Steve placed her in the front seat and buckled her in. It wasn't the first time but she sure hoped it would be the last. She stared out the side window the whole time he drove up the mountain. He kept reaching over and patting her thigh but he needed two hands on the wheel for most of the treacherous drive.

They pulled into his driveway but he didn't go into the garage. The plow on the front had pushed a drift of snow up to the garage door. He hopped out and walked around to her side. She fell against him when he opened the door and unbuckled her seatbelt.

"Come on, let's get you inside and I'll come back out and deal with the truck in a minute." He picked her up in his arms and walked through the snow to the front door.

How he managed to get the door unlocked and open and both of them inside without dropping her she didn't know. She heard the door close behind them and sighed in relief. The warmth of the house surrounded her and she shuddered.

"Cold? Want me to turn the heat up?" He strode down the hall to his room.

"No, it's fine."

"I'll run a bath. The warm water will be good for your sore muscles."

Steve set her on the closed toilet and turned on the bath taps. The tub was huge, made for two and the nozzles around the sides tempted her beyond reason.

"Can I turn the Jacuzzi on?"

"Definitely."

He helped her undress and into the bath. The water was

warm and she leaned back and let the heat seep into her skin and soothe her aches.

"I'll be back in five minutes. Don't let the water get above here." He pointed to the top of the jets.

"Okay."

Steve left and for the first time since she'd come to in the exam room she was completely alone. Her mind swirled with everything that had happened. She tried to retrace her steps, tried to work out if there was some other way things could have turned out. Gordie was relieved that Tatum and the babies were okay. There was no way she could have coped with that on her conscience.

She reached over to turn off the taps when the water rose above the silver jets. Lying back, she closed her eyes and willed herself to think of anything but today. Gordie hoped Steve returned soon or she'd fall to pieces. Startled by a noise behind her she sat up, her eyes opening wide.

"Sorry, should have made more noise coming through the bedroom. Didn't mean to frighten you." He stood next to the tub. Naked.

Gordie held up her hand. "Please." She didn't know what she was asking for but he seemed to understand what she needed.

He climbed in behind her and cradled her against his chest. When he pressed the button near his head the jets pulsed to life, the water and bubbles surging through them to pummel her from all sides. It was a gentle massage, rolling over aching muscles and tender bruises. Steve washed her with a soft, soapy cloth. Gentle strokes over sensitive skin.

When she was clean they lay back and enjoyed the spa bath. They stayed there until the water began to cool. The whole time he just held her close and drew small circles on her stomach with his fingertips. Suddenly the light touches weren't enough, she needed to feel him inside her, around her.

"Make love to me."

"Are you sure?" He stilled his movements. "You've been through a lot."

"I want to forget. Help me forget, Steve."

Steve stood, taking her with him. Water dripped from their bodies as he stepped out onto the mat. He didn't bother with towels, just strode out of the bathroom and over to the bed. Her back hit the soft quilt and Steve came down on top of her. She pulled his mouth to hers and thrust her tongue between his lips. Gordie tried to rush. Tried to dive deep into the mindless bliss being with him offered but he wouldn't let her.

He slowed her movements. Controlled her tongue with his and dragged her back to a leisurely pace. His hands stroked her body, soft, sweeping actions that nudged her closer and closer to the height of ecstasy. She tangled her fingers in the hair at his nape, ran her nails over his scalp and let him have his way.

They strolled up to the peak and when she fell from the edge he held her close and let her land in his waiting arms. He wedged his knee between hers and parted her legs. With a slow, easy glide, he slid inside her wet heat until he was buried deep. The ride was a gentle, calm journey back to the top. As they reached the summit he quickened the tempo, plunged harder, withdrew faster. Gordie gripped his shoulders, her fingers digging in to the tense muscles beneath his sweat-slick skin.

His mouth claimed hers in a kiss that mimicked the movements of their hips. Gordie lifted her legs and wrapped them around his waist, the change in angle allowing for deep penetration, more stimulation, and she was soon gasping for breath and rolling with the waves of her orgasm. Steve drove his cock to the hilt and came with her name on his lips.

They collapsed, exhausted, sweaty and well satisfied. He turned on his side, taking her with him, his softening length slipping from her body to rest between them. She waited to catch her breath, waited for the numbness to fade and real life to intrude once more but the day had taken a toll and she drifted to sleep before she could think about it anymore.

8

GORDIE ROLLED over and flinched in pain. In seconds, memories from the day before came rushing back to drown her in fear, desperation, anger and guilt. Emotions bombarded her, clouding her brain and twisting her insides. Her stomach pitched and she jumped from the bed to race for the bathroom. She made it just in time to dry heave into the toilet bowl. Her hollow belly contracted again and again. Steve came in behind her.

"Go away." She didn't want him to see her like this, couldn't bear for him to watch her when she lost control. It was going to happen. She could feel herself unraveling.

"No."

A warm cloth wiped across the back of her neck, over her forehead and she shivered at the contact. Her whole body trembled and her tummy continued to convulse in a vain attempt to expel something that wasn't there. She couldn't remember the last meal she'd eaten. All she knew for sure was she'd eat again and Marcus wouldn't.

"Don't, Gordie."

"Don't what?" She struggled to her feet, stood on shaky legs and tried to push past him.

"Blame yourself for Marcus' death." He blocked the doorway with his body.

"Don't blame myself?" She laughed, the sound harsh and grating to her ears. "How do I do that when I'm the one who killed him?"

"He was on a path of self-destruction. It could have been any one of us he came after with murder on his mind."

"But it wasn't." Her voice grew louder. "It was me!"

"Gordie." He reached for her but she brushed his hand aside.

"Don't you see?" she screamed. "This isn't me! It isn't who I am or what I stand for. I'm trained to save lives, not take them."

Gut-wrenching sobs broke free. She bent double, the pain ripping her in two. Her body shook violently as what she'd done tore at her very soul. Her knees gave out and she tumbled to the floor, arms wrapped around her middle in a desperate attempt to hold it together. Why now? Why did she have to give in to the grief, *the guilt,* now? She didn't want to lose control and fall apart in front of the one person she couldn't hide anything from.

Steve slipped to the floor beside her and scooped her back against his chest. Turning her, he cradled her in his warm embrace and rocked her like a child. The gentle care, the understanding and love that he gave her no matter how much she fought it enveloped Gordie and she cried harder for all that she'd lost. They'd lost.

"I can't stay," she sobbed.

He stilled beneath her. "What do you mean?"

"I can't live here. Can't live through the whispers again." She shook her head. "I can't."

"What whispers?"

"The pack. They'll talk behind my back like last time, whisper behind their hands whenever I'm near." She hiccupped as she tried to stifle another sob. "I couldn't live with it when Anthony died. Barely coped when I came back. Oh God."

"Stop." Steve tipped her face up and looked into her eyes. "No one will whisper behind your back and if they do, stiff shit. Who cares what they think or say? Your friends, your family, *me*, none of us will ever judge you for what happened yesterday. And you can bet every one of those men is wishing he'd been there to protect you. To save you from going through what you did. Especially me."

He closed his eyes, rested his forehead on hers and took a deep breath. "Gordie, what you did yesterday would affect the toughest of men and I know beyond a doubt that if there had been any other way to stop Marcus you would have. Killing him was the last resort. The only choice when push came to shove and it'll haunt me to my dying day that I wasn't there to do it for you."

His eyelids lifted. Moisture pooled in his eyes and sadness so great she hurt for him swam in the dark depths of his gaze. "Steve—"

"No." He placed a finger over her lips. "Don't say anything. Come back to bed and let me hold you for a while. I need to know you're safe. That you're here."

Gordie couldn't hold out against his obvious need. He'd given so much of himself and not just in the last few days. He'd been there in the background for years and she doubted she could find the strength to get through this without him. When they were together she was stronger, it seemed logical he would feel the same. They'd only just begun to explore a future and the idea of one without Steve made her heart ache—her stomach cramp.

"Take me back to bed."

She wasn't sure how she'd cope with the events of yesterday but for now she'd put that aside and be what he needed. What they needed.

STEVE HELD Doc while she slept. They'd been lying in the dark for hours but the first rays of sun were lighting up the sky now. The predicted storm had either missed them or not arrived yet. He glanced to the side, the digital readout on his clock showed six twenty-four. Too early to get up, too late to try for any more sleep. He sighed. Not that he'd been able to rest after she'd broken down.

Fear that she'd leave the mountains consumed him. Gnawed at his gut. He couldn't live without her. Not now that they'd connected. But he didn't see himself living anywhere but here. Whispering Springs was his home, building this house had been his dream, a dream he wanted to share with Gordie. His arms tightened around her and she snuggled closer. Should he take her acceptance of him in her most unguarded moment as a sign?

He stared through the skylight seeing nothing but dark rolling clouds as the daylight did its best to break through. Snow began to fall, light flurries that slid down the curved sheet of glass. Steve had designed the skylight himself, had the panel of toughened glass specially made. The majority of the house around them was handcrafted. From the timber beams supporting the roof and floors, to the furniture filling the rooms, he'd taken his dreams and turned them into reality.

"Why doesn't the snow stick to the glass?"

Steve hadn't realized Doc was awake. "The curved shape plus the house's heat rises to warm the panel from underneath. Small falls like this don't stick but if we get a good storm, more than a foot of snow on the ground, it'll cover the glass."

"You're not worried it will break?"

"No. That piece is specially designed, double glazed, you'd have to break it with a jackhammer."

"What else did you design?"

Her interest thrilled him but he didn't just want to tell her, he wanted to show. "Let's get dressed. We'll have something to eat and I'll give you the grand tour."

"Are you cooking?"

A niggle of fear pecked at his gut. Her voice was flat, devoid of any emotion and he wondered if it was an effect of the damage Marcus had done to her throat when he'd tried to choke the life out of her or if she'd clamped down on her feelings and shut him out again. "I'll cook."

He threw the covers back and rolled to the edge of the mattress. Sitting up, he scanned the floor for his pants before he remembered tossing the wet jeans in the wash last night. It suddenly dawned on him that Doc had no clothes. She'd come home in a hospital gown and the last thing on his mind had been to swing by her house to pick up the bag she'd packed. He hadn't washed in a week either, so the clothes she left the other day were still in the hamper.

"Damn." Steve stretched his back as he stood, glancing over his shoulder at Doc.

She'd pulled the quilt up under her armpits and leaned back on the headboard. "What's wrong?"

"I'm running out of clean clothes." He strode over to the dresser and rummaged around in the drawers. "I've got exactly three t-shirts, two pairs of jeans and one pair of sweatpants."

"I'll take a shirt and the sweatpants. I can put a load of washing on while you cook breakfast." She slipped from under the covers and got out of bed. With no regard for her nakedness, Doc walked toward him.

Steve groaned as he watched her breasts bounce with each step, his blood heated and his cock hardened. They'd made love twice during the night, the last time only a few hours ago and yet his body wanted more. He turned away, hoped "out of sight out of mind" worked. But it didn't stand a chance when her scent surrounded him and he could hear her pulling the shirt over her head, and picturing those gorgeous breasts being covered up did nothing to deflate his erection. He yanked on jeans and carefully pulled up the zipper.

"I take it you don't have any clean underwear either?" Doc pressed her lips to his back and slid her arms around his waist, her hands cool against his skin. "It's going to be awfully distracting knowing you've got nothing on under these things." She patted his cock through the thick denim.

"If you expect to eat any time soon you need to stop." Steve clenched his jaw and spoke through gritted teeth.

Gordie laughed and let go. "I need to use the bathroom. I'll meet you in the kitchen."

He turned his head, watched her walk away in his t-shirt, the sweatpants in her hand, and thought about following her. It wasn't as if they had to be anywhere. His stomach chose that moment to growl and remind him he hadn't eaten since yesterday morning. With a mental and physical shake, he cleared his mind of all sexy thoughts and finished getting dressed.

Steve detoured past the living room for a look at the deck. The snow continued to fall, growing heavier with each flake. Drifts collected on the north end and the wind picked up more snow and sent it flying in that direction as he watched. It looked as though the storm had arrived. A strong gust rattled the patio doors and it grew darker with every second.

He turned back to the room and searched for the remote so he could switch on the TV. Reception would be a problem soon but for now he should still be able to access the weather channel. What he saw didn't please him and he dropped the remote on the couch as he headed for the garage. He pulled out his snow gear and the tool he'd need to lower the snow guards fitted to the outside of each window. He stuck his head into the house and yelled for Gordie.

She came toward him at a run. Her feet were shoved into a pair of his work socks and she slid on the polished floor. "What? What's wrong?"

"Don't panic. I just wanted to let you know I'm heading outside to lower the window shutters. The storm is picking up and I don't want to risk a flying branch smashing any of them."

"Need help?"

"No, go on into the kitchen and put some coffee on. I'll only be a few minutes." He kissed her cheek. "I'll shut this door so the cold doesn't blow through when I open the roller door."

He closed the door and went to pull on his gear. With the wrench in his hand, he headed out into the growing storm. There had been no need to batten down the hatches before now so the shutters were still locked in their boxes. The guards were similar to a garage door but for windows, and once they were in place they'd keep out the cold as well as protect the glass.

It didn't take long and with all the boxes unlocked, he hurried back to the garage and the control pad that would lower all the shutters. Steve stripped out of his snowsuit and hung it up to dry. He double-checked the control panel before heading back inside the house.

Gordie had done more than make coffee. The scent of fried bacon and eggs greeted him when he opened the door between the garage and house. His mouth watered and he picked up the pace, his stomach rumbling with hunger. She was in front of the stove. His shirt covered her almost to her knees and the sweatpants had been rolled up so many times over her socked feet that she had to stand with her legs apart.

She shouldn't get him hot dressed like that. There was nothing sexy about her clothes or the way they hung off her body but Steve's cock had other ideas. His erection pressed against his fly, the cold metal zipper doing nothing to restrain its growth. With a moan he walked up behind her and wrapped her in his arms. He nibbled on her neck, licked at the red marks still visible on her skin and listened to the little whimpers of pleasure she made.

He hated knowing she'd been hurt. Hated being unable to take the pain away. But having her go soft in his arms went a long way to soothing his raw nerves. Steve rocked his hips, ground his throbbing cock against her lower back. She was a full head shorter than him and in this position he'd have to bend his knees to drive his length inside her. The idea made his blood surge, his pelvis buck and his balls ache. He'd like to take her in the kitchen, and every other room in the house, but first they needed to eat.

Steve groaned as he let her go and stepped back. He was gratified to hear a moan of need slip from her mouth. "Hold that thought, we'll get back to it." He patted her on the butt and headed for the coffee.

The spatula whacked him on the ass and he spilled coffee all over the counter as he yelped and spun around to face her. She held the utensil up, pointed at his chest.

"That was mean. You're a tease."

"A tease? I don't think so." He stepped toward her.

"Oh no you don't." She wagged the greasy spatula in his face. "The only thing you're getting now is breakfast."

He thought he heard her mumble "two can play that game"

but he wasn't sure and when she picked up the frying pan he chose not to question her just in case she hit him on the head with it, eggs and all. "I'll set the table."

Making a hasty retreat, Steve grabbed plates and cutlery and took them to the table. He went back for coffee and found Gordie hefting a large platter of bacon, toast and eggs. "Here. Give me that. You grab the coffee."

Steve took the tray and waited for her to pick up their mugs. She led the way and his gaze dropped to her butt wiggling beneath the baggy layer of clothes.

"Stop looking at my ass."

Startled, he barely missed tripping over his own feet. "I wasn't—"

"Yeah, you were. I saw you."

He brought his gaze up to meet hers. "You did?"

She grinned. "Yep. Now put the plate down and let's eat. I'm starving."

Steve kept his hands off her while they ate. Although how he did when she made eating breakfast more erotic than a strip-tease was beyond him. He managed only the occasional touch as they cleaned up which was a miracle considering she kept offering him a view of that perfect heart-shaped butt each time she bent to put a plate in the dishwasher. He wasn't at all sure he'd be as successful during the tour of the house. The idea of christening every room with Doc zapped his blood as though he'd shoved his finger in an electric socket.

GORDIE LISTENED TO STEVE, the pride clearly evident in his voice when he talked about the specially designed aspects of his house. They'd started with the upstairs area and she had to admit he'd planned the layout well. The living areas were separate from the bedrooms with no common walls to help cut down on noise transfer. She'd always known he was talented with timber but as she admired the handmade furniture and built-in cupboards in each room, she had to admit he was a genius.

She held the handrail on the stairs as they headed to the lower level. The timber felt smooth as silk under her fingers. Each rung beneath the rail was carved with intricate patterns that required closer inspection. Gordie bent to study them more carefully. When the details started to take shape before her eyes they surprised a delighted laugh out of her.

"What?" He stopped a few steps below her.

"They're coyotes frolicking in the forest. But they're so tiny you have to get right up to them to see." She glanced up at him. "I want you to make something for the clinic."

He smiled. "Sure. What did you have in mind?"

"I don't know. I don't care." She trailed her fingertips over the tail of a coyote. "I just want something this beautiful there."

Steve laughed and leaned over to brush her mouth with his. To her disappointment, he pulled away before the kiss could lead anywhere.

"Come on, I want to know what you think about my plans for down here. It's a work in progress." He held her hand and walked through the open area. "This will have a pool table and the bar will be over there. I'm waiting on a special piece of timber for the top of that half wall."

Gordie could imagine the large space lined with comfy chairs and couches while the pool table took up center stage. "You'll need some plush seating around the edges. And the barstool seats should match the couches."

"Exactly." He pulled her over to a doorway on the wall next to the bar. "This will be a movie room. I've got one of those big screens in mind for that far wall and rows of seats back here. I figure this room will get a workout on days like today when the kids are snowed in and driving us nuts."

"Kids?"

"Sure. Don't you want any?"

"But I'm not—"

"Don't say it. Forget about leaving, forget yesterday. Think only of tomorrow and it's wide open. You're free to go after your heart's desire." He cupped her face, his thumbs stroking her cheeks. "What does your heart want, Gordie?"

Gordie's nose tingled with the tears she refused to shed. She could see a future with him. See their children running through the house, playing in the forest out back. His gaze searched hers and she couldn't hide what was in her heart from that all-seeing gaze of his.

"You want it, I know you do. It's yours for the taking, Gordie. All you have to do is stay."

"I can't." The first tear slipped from her lashes. "I couldn't handle the stares and whispers after Anthony died and I didn't kill him."

He rubbed his thumb over the moisture on her face. "I know it hurt before, but Gordie, you were grieving, you'd lost your husband, your baby, everything hurt. It wasn't the looks or the words that sent you running. It was your broken heart."

On some level she knew he was right, knew removing herself from her home had been the only way to cope with the loss she'd suffered. She'd distracted herself as best she could, immersed herself in her studies, had no life other than classes and books and then her internship. It took years to find the strength to come home but from the first day she arrived back in Whispering Springs she knew it had been the right time to return. The mountains were her home, had always been home and her coming back had never really been in question. How much of that had to do with this man?

Gordie wrapped her arms around his waist and buried her face in his chest. She cried silently, her tears soaking the front of his shirt, the salty taste coating her lips and tongue. He held her without speaking, let her take the time she needed and right there she knew she'd never be able to leave him and stay whole. No matter where she went or what she did he'd keep a piece of her with him and neither of them would ever find true happiness.

The crying jag slowed and she continued to lean against him, absorbing his warmth and strength. Gordie had no idea what would happen once word got out about Marcus, didn't want to speculate about the pack's reaction. Many were still loyal to the Connellys, and even with the events over the past year, they had allies. Whether they'd cause trouble was anyone's guess. She just hoped that now the last Connelly was gone, the pack could prosper.

She tilted her head back to look at Steve through tear-drenched eyes. "I'm worried about those sympathetic to Marcus."

He brushed the hair off her forehead. "I doubt any of them will be a problem. Most are old men and caught in a time long gone. Without a reminder they'll soon forget."

"God, I hope so."

"Even if they don't, Brogan isn't about to let the pack suffer and I'm certainly not going to let anyone hurt you if I can help it. I can't stop the talk but I can help you hold your head high and live here in peace."

"I'm not sure I'll ever find peace."

"You will. I'll make sure of it." He bent down and brushed her lips with his. "That's a promise."

Steve deepened the kiss. His tongue licked across her mouth and pushed inside. He tasted of bacon and coffee, and Gordie moaned as his tongue stroked over hers. She slipped her hands under the hem of his shirt and palmed his warm flesh. They pressed closer, their bodies touching, but the height difference proved awkward and restricted their contact. Frustrated, she pulled her mouth from his.

"More. I need more," she panted.

He picked her up, carried her out of the unfinished movie room and across to the stairs. With ease, he made the journey up to the main floor. His long strides ate up the distance to his bedroom quickly. In a second, he'd tossed her on the mattress and followed her down. She tore at his clothes, stretched his shirt to get him out of the barrier between her skin and his. Steve did the same to hers. With frenzied actions they stripped each other and were soon rolling naked on the bed.

Gordie ended up on top, straddling his thighs. Her fingers curled around his cock and she pumped her hand up and down in slow, loose strokes. His hips lifted, thrusting his rigid length into her grip.

"Harder." Steve wrapped his hand around hers and squeezed. "Tighter."

Guided by him, she dragged her hand over his silky shaft. Liquid beaded on the head and she leaned down to taste it. His scent filled her nostrils, his salty flavor coated her tongue and the need to take all of him gripped her. She opened her mouth, slipped her lips around the bulbous head and sucked. Gordie took him to the back of her throat and swirled her tongue along his shaft.

Steve groaned, the sound ended on a growl and his fingers twisted in her hair. He held her still and plunged his cock between her lips in short, sharp jabs. His hips jerked, his length pulsing against her tongue and more of his musky flavor filled her mouth. Gordie breathed through her nose and increased her suction. She gasped when he yanked her hair, pulled free of her mouth and tugged her up his body.

"Ride me."

She didn't need convincing. Gordie wanted to feel his length filling her core. Wanted his heat pounding into her until she saw stars. Steve held her waist and she used her hand to guide his cock to her opening. The crown rubbed over her clit, sending shards of fire into her pussy. Moisture covered her folds and he slid between them with ease, entering her in one smooth stroke.

Gordie tossed her head back and moaned. His flesh branded hers, the heat scorching a trail as it blazed out to invade every nerve, overpower ever sense. She surrendered, body and soul she gave herself up to the sensations of being joined with him. He jerked under her, his hips bucking off the bed to start the delicious friction that would drive them wild.

Time stood still as she rocked into him, slid her body over his in sensuous glides. She rose up, dropped down, rolled her pelvis and ground her clit against him. Each move delivered another blast of fire, turned her core into a molten mass desperate for release. He pulled her down and latched his mouth around her nipple. A jolt of electricity struck her, bowed her body and drove his cock deeper. Gordie cried out, hung on the razor's edge of orgasm for what seemed like forever.

Steve sucked on her breast, drew on the peak before scraping the puckered bud with his teeth. He bit down. Pain and pleasure clashed and Gordie flew into the abyss. Her breath stalled in her lungs, her mind splintering in a million different directions as pure bliss saturated her senses. The world spun and she found herself beneath him, his body slamming into hers as muscles grasped greedily at his cock.

He rammed into her, pressed on her clit with every plunge and propelled her over a second peak. Her name burst from his lips as he came. His body bucked against hers, the spasms rolling from one to the other as their orgasms joined as effectively as their bodies. Wave after wave of heat and pleasure swamped her. She gasped for air and scratched at his back, desperate for solid ground.

Gordie slowly drifted back to earth. Caught between Steve and the mattress, she savored the feeling of satisfaction, contentment. He made her feel cherished, wanted, *loved*. And with all those came strength. Determination to have what should be hers. Take what should be theirs. She wouldn't walk away from him, couldn't if she were honest.

"I love you." The words surprised her. She hadn't even thought them and they'd tripped off her tongue as easily as her breath.

Waiting for a response just about killed her. He'd gone so still and she wasn't sure he'd taken a breath since she'd spoken. She pushed against his chest but he was as movable as a brick wall.

Gordie sighed and slumped into the bed. "Say something."

"I can't. I've waited forever to hear those words from you. Let me enjoy them a minute more."

She slapped his arm. "You idiot. It won't be the only time I say them."

"No, but this will always be the first time."

"At least one of us is getting a first today." Gordie couldn't believe the pouty voice she used. She sounded like a three-year-old sulking after being denied a cookie.

Steve lifted his head and stared at her. "You're pouting, Doc. It doesn't suit you. Besides, it's not necessary. I love you. I've always loved you. I will love you forever." He leaned down and kissed her.

They took it slow, lips meshing, tongues sliding, they rejoiced in the freedom of acceptance. When the kiss ended, Gordie opened her eyes and stared at the naked need in his gaze. A growl echoed from deep inside and she knew what she had to do. One final step.

"I want to run."

He reared back. "It's snowing."

"I know. But I need to run."

Rolling to his back, he took her with him. "You'll have to wait for the run but we could shift now. See what happens."

Gordie curled into his side. "Would you mind? It's been months since I changed and I feel her clawing to be free. I've never had that before."

"Want to do it now or later? I'm thinking a nap might be nice about now."

"It can wait. She's settled now that I've decided to run." Gordie yawned. "And a sleep would be good."

"Then sleep it is. We don't have to be anywhere and with the storm blowing like it is even if we did we wouldn't be going. Look up."

She glanced up at the skylight. The glass dome was completely covered in snow. "Oh. It's a bad one then."

"Yeah, I don't think we'll be driving out of here anytime soon, but if the snow stops falling we'll take a run in the forest."

Gordie yawned again. "Okay." She drifted to sleep in the comfort of his arms.

IT TOOK two days for the snow to stop falling long enough for Steve to be happy about going outside. He'd put her off as long as he could but he'd given in this afternoon. The sun was starting to dip toward the mountain and he wanted to be inside before it dropped behind the ridge and they lost daylight. They were in the garage. The house was locked up and he stripped out of his clothes and shifted quickly to escape the cold.

Doc stood near the door. She wrung her hands and he thought she'd changed her mind about running. She took a deep breath and grabbed the hem of the sweatshirt she wore. In a flash she had the top up and off, and was stepping out of her pants. It took her longer than him to shift, but not so long that he panicked. Her coat was a mix of grays and whites woven in a tapestry of thick strands.

Like her human form, her coyote was small, about half the size of his. He trotted over, nuzzled her face and nipped at her side. She danced away, danced back and he butted her with his head to get her moving. Her bark surprised him but he answered and took off out the garage door.

They ran. Sometimes he led, sometimes he followed. He chased her, wrestled her to the ground and let her go. The air was clear and crisp, the snow fresh and soft, and his heart pounded with the beat of his paws as they raced back to the house. Steve slowed down to a walk and took the last few feet to the garage at a stroll. Doc kept pace with him and they went inside together.

She shook, water and snow flying every which way and he quickly joined her. Even with their coats of fur, the cold was starting to settle in. It might have stopped snowing and the sun might be shining but it was still chilly enough to freeze them in moments if they didn't hurry. He shifted and reached for the towels he'd brought out before their run. Steve dried himself and waited for Doc to change.

"Hurry up. It's freezing out here." He held the second towel out for her to step into once she'd shifted to human form.

He watched her closely and realized something wasn't right. She'd lain down on her side and was panting heavily. Panic spiked but he reeled it in and went to her. Steve used the towel to pat her down and soak up some of the dampness. Her eyes drooped and it all fell into place.

Doc hadn't run in months, hadn't shifted in just as long and they'd been out in the winter air for a good hour. She was too tired to shift. He draped the towel over her and picked her up to carry her inside. Going straight to the bedroom, Steve laid her on the bed and finished drying her.

"Have a sleep. You'll be fine as soon as you've rested." The words were for his benefit as much as hers.

She yipped softly and licked his face. He tossed both towels at the bathroom and crawled onto the bed beside her. Her coat drew his fingers and he combed the fur behind her ears until her eyes closed and soft snores came from her throat. The thought of leaving her never entered his mind and he lay watching her sleep for long moments before drifting off himself.

THE PHONE WOKE HIM. He sat up and reached for the bedside receiver. Obviously the lines had been repaired this afternoon. He'd checked before their run and found dead air. Steve glanced at the clock. Six thirty. They'd been asleep about an hour.

"Hello." He turned to look at Doc. At some point she'd shifted back to human form and lay on her stomach with her head buried in her pillow.

"Hey, Steve." Kat's voice came through crystal clear. "Just checking the two of you are still alive up there."

"We're fine." He sighed and leaned against his pillow.

"Thought you would be, but I promised Mom I'd call."

"Doc would have rung but the lines have been down since Christmas night," he said.

"The crews have been working like mad to get everything

back up. Good thing I've got that generator out back or I'd have lost a truckload of food these past two days."

"The town lost power? Wow, it was a big storm."

"Not real bad, more bad luck, I think. The big old tree over near the substation came down, took out the power and they would have had it up and running quicker if the snow had stopped falling sooner."

"Anyone hurt?"

"No, nobody's stupid enough to go out in this weather."

He could hear someone talking in the background and Kat's whispered "give me a second".

"Are you at the café?" Steve asked.

"Yeah, Mom and Dad are here too. We were wondering if you guys would be able to head down here for dinner in the next few days."

"Probably be another day or two and that's only if the snow holds off."

"Well you'll be pleased to know they're not predicting another storm until after the first of the year. Hang on a sec, Steve."

There was some shuffling of the phone followed by what sounded like an argument and then Mrs. Monroe spoke.

"Steven McKenna, you get yourself and my daughter down here the minute you can. I want to see both of you within the next two days or I'll drive up there."

More shuffling and Kat was back. "Sorry." Her sigh sounded like wind blowing through the line. "I tried to hold her off. She's got some bee in her bonnet about you two getting married on New Year's Eve because she and Dad are planning to leave on the first."

"What?" He glanced at Doc, found her watching him intently. "Um, I'm not so sure about that, Kat."

"Not sure? That's not what you said the other day."

"No, that's not what I mean. I'm sure about the getting married part, it's the when that's uncertain."

Doc sat up and arched one eyebrow.

"Have you two even talked about a date?" Kat asked.

"Not specifically. Look, Kat, I'll talk to Doc, but no matter what your mother wants it won't happen if Doc's not ready."

"I get that but you'll have to tell it to Mom. The woman is driving both me and Dad batty." Kat dropped her voice to a whisper. "I think she's frightened Gordie will change her mind and run again."

He laughed. "Doc has never run from anything in her life."

"Yes, she has. She ran away after Anthony died and we didn't see her for months on end."

Steve sobered. "Kat, she wasn't running from anything. She was running *to* something. Doc needed to find herself and she couldn't do that here." He watched Doc as he spoke to her sister. Saw surprise cross her face, fill her eyes.

"But what's to stop her from doing that again?" Kat argued.

"Me." It was simple really, love and trust would keep her beside him. "Look, I've gotta go. We'll call and let you know when we're coming to town."

Steve leaned over and hung up the phone, never taking his eyes off Doc's. He couldn't read what she was thinking but he knew she was. That sexy over-thinking brain of hers was all but smoking as she tried to work her way through his half of the conversation.

"How did you know that?"

"What?"

"That I wasn't running away when I left here?"

He shrugged. "You're not a coward, Doc. Running would never occur to you."

"But *I* thought I was running."

"I never saw it that way. Before you married Anthony your

plans were to go away to school, it seemed logical to go ahead with the plan after the accident. It gave you a focus, a dream you'd always had you could make come true." He reached over and threaded his fingers into the hair at her nape, tugged her closer. "What other dreams do you have, Doc?"

Steve leaned in and kissed her. He flicked his tongue along the seam of her mouth and applied pressure until she let him in. His caresses were feather soft, not demanding, just offering. She had all of him, held his heart—*his soul*—in the palm of her hand. Freely given, no strings. Take it or leave it, her decision wouldn't matter, he was hers until the day he died.

He rolled her beneath him. Took the kiss deeper and savored the feel of her body melting into his. Her breasts were crushed to his chest, her nipples hardening as he rubbed against her. She moaned into his mouth and he drew the sound in, swallowed it whole. They arched together, his sex pressed to hers and the give became take. Neither of them had put their clothes back on after their run so there was only skin on skin.

Heat and need rolled through him. Pulled his balls up tight and made his cock throb. He tilted his hips, slid his length along her slit and reveled in the moisture that coated his flesh. She writhed below him, her hot folds gripping his shaft, dragging him deeper into the maelstrom of sensations bombarding him.

Her mouth left his, her teeth nibbling a trail down his chin, his throat. "Love me."

"I do."

"No. Make love to me. Now." She bit his shoulder, her tongue soothing the sting with one long lick.

Steve leaned back, stared down at the woman under him and wondered if he could ever deny her a thing. "With pleasure."

She spread her legs, wrapped them around his waist and dug her heels into the backs of his thighs to pull him inside her.

He flexed his hips, brought his cock to her entrance and thrust deep. Her walls gloved him, scorched him with liquid fire and drove him to the edge of sanity. Passion flared, exploded in a burst of wicked wanting that stole every other thought from his mind except claiming Gordie.

He drove into her again and again. Thrusting to the hilt and withdrawing to the crown on each stroke. She bucked and thrashed, her body meeting his in need and demand. Her teeth grazed his throat, sank into his shoulder and he nipped at her ear, licked and sucked and bit until she moaned against his skin.

"Steve." Harsh, hot breath coated his neck. "I want. *Need.*"

"What?" he panted. "What do you need, Gordie, what do you want?"

She arched under him and he sank deeper inside her, farther into the inferno consuming them. Her pussy squeezed him, gripped and released him in a punishing vise that stole his breath.

"*You,*" she screamed.

The orgasm detonated between them with such violence Steve lost control. His hips jerked, his balls imploded and blasted shot after shot of cum through his shaft. Fire licked up his spine and erupted to shower him from head to toe in ecstasy. He collapsed on top of her, all energy incinerated by their joining.

"*Fuck.*"

Doc's lips curled on his shoulder. "Yeah, that fits."

"Jesus. Give me second."

"I want to stay."

He lifted his head, looked down at Doc's flushed face. "Was there ever any doubt?"

"For me, yes." She closed her eyes, took a deep breath that raised her chest, pressed her breasts against him. Her lids lifted to reveal tears. "I don't want to promise something I might not be able to give. I don't know if I can do it, but I want to."

"You don't have to know. Life doesn't hold guarantees, Gordie. All I ask is that you let me love you, love me in return and promise to never hold anything back again. No matter how trivial or how inconvenient something is, I want to know about it." He searched her gaze. "Can you give me that?"

"Yes." She kissed him quickly. "So you want to get married on New Year's Eve?"

Steve smiled. "I'll marry you whenever you want. I'd get dressed and plow our way to town now if you wanted."

"Really?"

"Yeah, really."

"Okay, let's go." She tried to push him off her.

He laughed, rolled to his side and pulled her with him. "New Year's Eve is good enough if that's what you really want. Besides, as far as I'm concerned we're as good as married now."

She laid her head on his chest, her fingers playing over his skin. "Steve?"

"Mmm."

"This is my dream."

EPILOGUE

THE CLOSER THEY got to town the harder her heart pounded. She could suck in no more than shallow gasps of air and sweat coated her skin, especially her palms. Her fingers trembled along with her stomach. Gordie just hoped she didn't embarrass herself and throw up the second she got out of the truck.

Steve's hand landed on her thigh. "Stop worrying. Everything will be fine."

"You can't know that."

"Yes, I can." He glanced her way, turned back to watch the road. "We have each other, don't we?"

"Yes, but—"

"See, everything is fine."

She took a deep breath. "That's not what has me nervous and you know it."

He patted her leg. "Gordie, you did what you had to, there was no other choice and those that matter to you, to us, know that."

They turned a bend and the town came into view. It

looked exactly the same as it had every other time she'd traveled this road. On the surface nothing had changed. But on the inside, like her, nothing was the same. Steve drove through the center of town, found a spot across the street from the café and parked. He switched off the engine and turned toward her.

"If you don't want to do this now, would prefer to wait, we can."

"What?" She spun in her seat. "No. I want to get married. I've wanted it for days. What I don't want is to face the people waiting for us in there." She indicated her sister's café.

"The only people here are the ones we invited, our family and friends. None of them are going to judge you." He unbuckled both their belts and pulled her across the console as he opened his door. "Come on, let's go change your last name."

Gordie laughed. "Is that all we're doing?"

"Did I mention you'll be tied to me for life?"

She shook her head.

"Probably best to leave that until after we change your name then." He grinned and pulled her out of the truck behind him.

"What other secrets have you kept hidden?" They linked hands and checked for traffic before heading across the road.

"Oh, a lifetime of happiness, a houseful of children, getting old and wrinkly together." Steve put his hand on the door to Kat's place. "Ready?"

"And willing."

The noise from a party well underway greeted them. Kat came rushing over yelling above those already inside.

"They're here." She linked arms with each of them, separating them. "Let's get this show on the road."

Her sister led them to a small flower-festooned arch that had been place in front of the big stone fireplace at the back of the room. William Brant stood in a creaseless suit waiting to commence the ceremony.

"Gordie, Steve, lovely to see you both."

Steve shook the older man's hand. "Thanks for doing this on such short notice."

"Nonsense. It's my pleasure." William turned to Gordie. "Shall we start?"

"Yes."

They removed their coats and stood facing each other, their hands joined. Everyone moved in around them and a hush fell over the room. The vows were simple and in only a few sentences she was Dr. Gordana McKenna. Steve bent down to kiss her. A soft brush that was nowhere near enough. She wrapped her arms around his neck, pulled herself up on her toes and showed Steve what a real kiss should be like. Breathless, she gulped for air while whistles and applause rang in her ears.

He grinned at her. "Hello, Mrs. McKenna."

"That's Dr. McKenna to you."

His smile grew bigger. "Doc McKenna. Oh yeah, I like that even better."

Steve picked her up and spun around. Gordie tossed her head back and laughed. He put her down and they were surrounded.

Congratulatory hugs and kisses were delivered by all before Kat called an end to the ceremony and a beginning to the wedding feast.

Her mother cried. Silent, happy tears she reassured everyone but she continued to sniffle through the meal and Gordie sat beside her, holding her hand and talking. When everyone was stuffed full to the gills Brogan got up and made a speech. He kept it short but he did get in a dig at Steve for taking so long to chase her down. With the formal part of the wedding over a few people left but others stayed well into the afternoon and she sat back and enjoyed the rest of the day.

STEVE WATCHED HIS WIFE.

Jesus. His wife.

He'd wished and hoped and prayed for so long he still wasn't sure it was real. Doc laughed at something Rowan said. The women had been sitting together deep in conversation for well over an hour and he had a feeling most of the discussion centered on the coming babies. Tatum got up and headed over to Dale. She whispered in his ear and they both looked in his direction before she returned to the table.

He wasn't surprised when Dale walked over to stand beside him. The topic the sheriff brought up did shock him though.

"We went over the clinic with a fine-toothed comb. I know how he was getting in and out and where he's been hiding all these weeks."

Steve turned to look at Dale. "Marcus? Where?"

"It looks like he was hiding out in the roof cavity of the clothing shop next door. He removed some paneling to get into the clinic's roof space. From there he just had to drop in through the manhole like he did at the house."

"Son of a bitch."

"Doctor Monroe has organized to have the roofing checked and repaired. The deputies cleared out all the evidence and the rubbish so Gordie doesn't have to worry about that," Dale said.

"Why are you telling me this today?"

"Because I figured I'd rather you tell her about it before she opens up the clinic day after tomorrow."

"Coward."

"There's more."

"More? What more could there be?" Steve asked.

"His brother's coming home to claim the body."

"What?" Steve glanced around, dropped his voice so no one would hear. "Brady hasn't been seen in, shit, over ten years. Everyone figured old man Connelly killed him and Mrs. Connelly the year the Wilders were killed in that mountain accident."

"Well apparently the boy, man now I guess, is alive and well. And to make it even more interesting, Brogan hired him on as a wilderness guide and from what our sovereign says, Brady Connelly is definitely home to stay."

"Great. Just great."

Tatum walked toward them ending the conversation.

"Ready to go?" Dale asked her.

She covered a yawn with one hand while pressing the other into her back causing her pregnant belly to bulge even more. "We were ready an hour ago but we couldn't miss out on this special day."

Tatum waddled closer to him and tried to stretch up to kiss his cheek. "Jeez, help a girl out, Steve, bend down here." He leaned forward and she planted a kiss on him. "I'd say make her happy but I know you will so instead I'll say I hope the scientists work out how men can carry babies before you two decide to have children and you get to do this part."

He laughed and hugged her to his side. "If I haven't said it before now, Tatum, welcome home. I think having you around will lead to interesting times." He eyed Dale as the other man fidgeted beside them.

"Thank you. I'm really happy to be back. Come on, sheriff. Let's go home." She linked her arm with Dale's and ambled toward the door.

Doc came up next to him and slipped her arm around his

waist. "Do you think we'll know what the deal is with those two anytime soon?"

"It's inevitable in this small town." Steve tugged her around in front of him. "So, are you ready to go home, Doc McKenna?"

"Yes," she sighed and laid her cheek on his chest. "I'm exhausted and I've done nothing but sit on my butt all day and talk."

"Well I'm sure flapping those sexy lips takes energy." He bent to plant a kiss on said lips. "You can nap in the truck because there's no way I'm letting you sleep through our wedding night. I've got plans for you, Dr. McKenna."

"Oh, sounds intriguing but I've got some plans of my own."

"Really?" He arched an eyebrow. "And just what might those be?"

She stood on tiptoes, put her mouth to his ear and whispered.

Chapter 1

January 15

BRADY SUCKED in a breath when he rounded the bend and the first buildings came into view.

Whispering Springs.

The place he'd been born.

Eyes scanning, he eased off the gas, and took in the changes.

Here, on the outer edges of town, things looked the same. Mostly. There had definitely been changes, minor ones—new paint, some additions—but nothing stood out too much. He was sure he'd see more once he got to the middle of town but right here, on the outskirts of the town he'd grown up in, it was as though he hadn't spent over a decade living somewhere else.

A wave of comfort flowed over him.

Home.

He'd finally come home.

The years away didn't matter; in his heart he knew this was home.

Would always be home.

He'd sought out every piece of information he could before taking the job with Wild Encounters and making the journey here. The owners, Brogan Wilder and Quinn MacClellan, had intrigued him for a number of reasons. They'd managed to build a reputable company that offered wilderness adventures to shifters and humans unlike anything he'd come across in the region or the country for that matter.

Through discreet inquiries Brady also knew they were well on their way to bringing life back to an almost decimated coyote population. Both the natural packs that roamed this mountain range and the shifter pack who called Whispering Springs and surrounding mountains home.

As sovereign and regal of the Whispering Mountain coyote shifters, the two men had strengthened the pack Brady had always thought of as his in spite of not living within its midst these last thirteen years.

His chest ached, his stomach churned, bile rising up his throat, as he thought about his father's involvement in the near destruction of the once prosperous Whispering Mountain pack.

Thinking of his father always turned his insides. Brady couldn't remember much about the man from his early years, and his mother always insisted things hadn't been as bad as their final years living on the mountain, except it didn't seem to matter how much his mother said his father had once been a better man because Brady only remembered a man with a temper, a man whose anger simmered constantly and only took a small infraction—real or perceived—to set off.

Memories of the night they fled flashed through his mind.

His father's rage before he'd stormed out of the house leaving bruises behind. His mother throwing things in bags, racing from room to room taking very few of their possessions, before finally ushering them outside. Marcus, refusing to get in the car. The fear and desperation radiating from his mother as she frantically argued with her oldest son. Her vain attempts to drag Marcus into their beat-up old truck.

From what Brady could remember, his older brother had

been stubborn and had idolized their father; his refusal to leave hadn't come as a surprise, but Marcus calling their mother a traitor and a whore had.

Brady had never wanted to hurt someone as badly as he had that night. He'd wanted to punch his brother in the face until he shut up and did what their mom wanted. Especially after she'd given up and climbed behind the wheel, her gaze fixed on the road ahead, never once looking back at the son she left behind.

She'd cried the whole fourteen hours she drove. Silent tears that streamed down her face and soaked her shirt.

He had never felt more useless or terrified in his life. At fourteen he'd been too young to defend her against his brute of a father but he had succeeded in avoiding confrontations during his early teens, protecting her as best he could by not setting off his father's rage. His efforts had never been enough.

Everything had come crashing down around them the night they left. The whole world had shifted beneath his feet with one act of violence his mother couldn't ignore.

Malcolm Connelly would stop at nothing to gain sovereign. Not even murder.

Ironic how murder had driven Brady out of the mountains and murder brought him back.

A heavy sigh left his chest; the weight of all he faced sat on his shoulders like his favorite hiking pack. A burden he had no choice but to carry. Not if he wanted to stay. And he wanted to stay.

He didn't know what kind of reception he would receive from the pack members, especially after recent events, but he hadn't expected coming home to be easy. Not after the way he and his mother had fled. With a deep breath, he straightened his spine and focused on the town that as of today would be his home once more.

Punching the accelerator, he shot forward with a little more haste than necessary and drove toward his future.

In less than a minute he was driving down the town's main street. Slowing to walking pace, he scrutinized the shops lining the road, seeing familiar stores as he headed toward the Den Cafe. The cafe had been a fundamental part of life in Whispering Springs from before Brady was born. It didn't only serve great food, it served as a meeting point, a social outing, a place for pack members to congregate, to catch up, and, for the older generation, a place to gossip.

It wasn't surprising that Brogan had suggested Brady meet him and Quinn there. He remembered them both from before he left but he wasn't sure if they remembered him. They had to have recognized his name though.

No one had mentioned who he was—or the other reason for his return to the mountains—during his interview but they knew he'd grown up in Whispering Springs. They'd spoken on the phone several times over the last few weeks and Brady felt comfortable accepting the position with their adventure company even if returning to the mountain left him with a mix of anxiety and excitement.

Funny how something he'd longed for for years could bring such conflicting emotions.

On the one hand, he couldn't wait to return to the town he loved and missed. On the other, he feared the very people he'd thought of as family for the first fourteen years of his life. *Still* thought of that way if he were honest.

The cafe came into view and Brady quickly searched the street for a parking spot. Seeing one just beyond his destination, he sped up and slipped his truck between two off-road vehicles. He set the parking brake and turned the engine off except he didn't get out.

Muscles taut and chest heavy as though a weight pressed

down on it, crushing the air from his lungs, he took a moment to get himself together. After several deep breaths, Brady grunted. With determination and a small amount of self-disgust, he yanked the keys from the ignition and popped his door.

Since the night his mother took him from his home, he'd vowed to never let fear stop him. And in the last thirteen years he'd kept that promise. He wasn't about to break it now.

He'd already broken the one he'd given his mother on her deathbed. Not that he could have done otherwise. He hadn't had anything to do with his brother in over decade and even he wasn't stupid enough to think he could have changed the outcome of his brother's life by making contact sooner.

No, his brother's destiny had been set in motion all those years ago when Marcus had chosen to stay with their father instead of leaving with their mother.

With more force than warranted, Brady shoved his door wide and climbed out. Slamming it shut behind him, he locked the truck and headed for the Den Cafe.

Encountering no one on the sidewalk, he breathed in and out, slow and steady, his stride becoming more relaxed with each breath of crisp mountain air and step he took.

Only a thin layer of snow crunched beneath his boots. It had been days since the last snowfall, but it was still the middle of winter in Whispering Springs and crisp was a polite way to say the air froze your nose hairs and cracked your lungs.

The temperature might be mild today, the sky a blinding winter-blue, but it was still bone-chillingly cold.

In spite of the cold and his apprehension, Brady felt the town—his home—seeping into his bones, embracing his soul, and warming his heart.

Glancing up and down the street, he smiled.

God, it was good to be home.

Not one to hide his head in the sand, he didn't think for a

second that this was anything except the calm before the storm. There would be plenty to face the minute the townspeople realized who he was. He was prepared to meet whatever they threw at him; he'd come home for good, and no matter what his brother and father had done in the past, it wouldn't stop him from being here and claiming his place in the pack of his birth.

A bell jingled above his head as he pushed through the door. The sounds of people chatting, utensils scratching on plates, hit him like a brick wall, and he smiled at the homey feel of the cafe. Stepping inside, he shut the door, blocking out the cold, and scanned the tables for Brogan and Quinn.

As his gaze passed each group, silence followed as though an invisible soundproof blanket was being laid over the room. By the time he'd located the two men he sought in a back booth, you could hear a pin drop even without the added bonus of shifter hearing.

Brady stiffened his spine and returned the smiles of the men waving him over. With deliberate steps and head high, he moved in their direction; clamping down on the anxiety eating a hole in his gut, he kept the smile on his face and his gaze on target.

He'd made it halfway across the room when it hit him.

Raw, scraping need stole the breath from his lungs and snapped every muscle in his body rigid, tore at his nerves with razor sharp edges.

What the fuck?

His groin pulsed and his cock grew hard from one heartbeat to the next. He'd left his jacket in the truck and the sweater he wore barely skimmed his hips; his jeans, old favorites, hid nothing if someone were to look. God, he hoped nobody looked.

Clenching his jaw and eyes focused straight ahead, he

moved as quick as his locked muscles allowed toward the far booth and the men he'd come to meet.

Reaching the table he held out a hand to the pack's sovereign and his new boss. "Brogan."

"Brady." Brogan's grip was strong, confident. "You made good time."

"I did." Turning to the other owner of Wild Encounters and the pack's regal, Brady offered his hand again. "Quinn."

"Brady, good to have you here," Quinn said with a quick shake.

Brogan motioned for Brady to take a seat and he slid into the booth as both men took the bench seat opposite.

"Did most of the driving at night. Plus I got away earlier than I'd planned from Nebraska," he explained. "Once I made up my mind to make the move, I wanted to get here. Get started."

He jerked in his seat as another wave of lust slammed into him. His gaze skimmed the room but he couldn't pinpoint the woman who had to be here.

"Something wrong?" Quinn asked.

"Huh?" He brought his gaze back to the men across the table. "No. No. Just taking the place in. It's not all that different from the last time I was here."

Brady hoped neither man saw through his lie. Not that the place had changed, that part wasn't the lie, but he hadn't lived in a pack since leaving Whispering Springs at fourteen; he couldn't tell if they were able to sense his deception—his discomfort.

He'd been around other shifters over the years and in spite of his mother's assertions not all coyote shifters were like his father, they had never joined another pack. She hadn't left his heritage in the past though; she'd told him about every aspect of being a coyote so he knew what was happening right now even if he wasn't sure what to do about it.

Never in a million years did he think he'd find his mate the first day he came back to town.

Except coyote instincts didn't lie, and right now his were screaming his mate was right here.

In the Den Cafe.

ABOUT THE AUTHOR

Rhian Cahill is the alter ego of a former stay-at-home mother of four. With motherly duties rapidly dwindling Rhian is able to make use of the fertile imagination she used to keep herself sane for all those years of slavery. Having spent years living overseas and visiting tropical climates has helped inspire some steamy stories.

Multi-published in erotic romance and contemporary romance, Rhian, with the help of Mr. Muse, spends her days and nights writing.

When not glued to the keyboard you'll find her book or knitting in hand avoiding any and all housework as much as possible.

For more on Rhian –

Website – http://www.rhiancahill.com/
Newsletter signup – http://www.rhiancahill.com/contact/newsletter/
Twitter – https://twitter.com/RhianCahill
FaceBook – https://www.facebook.com/RhianCahillAuthor
Instagram – http://instagram.com/rhiancahill/
BookBub – https://www.bookbub.com/authors/rhian-cahill
Goodreads page - https://www.goodreads.com/rhian_cahill

LOOK FOR THESE TITLES BY RHIAN CAHILL

Boys Of Summer

Bondi Beach Boys

Sand, Surf And Sunnie

Coyote Hunger Series

Coyote Home – Book 1

Coyote Wild – Book 2

Coyote Whispers – Book 3

Coyote Law – Book 3.5

Coyote Lies – Book 4

Party Games Series

Truth Or Dare

Spin The Bottle

Pass The Parcel – Novella

Are You Game Series

7 Minutes In Heaven – Book 1

Catch'n'Kiss – Book 2

Red Light, Green Light – Book 3

For a full list of Rhian's available books visit her website

http://www.rhiancahill.com/books/